THE TROUBLE WITH CHARLIE

"Tell me more about your sisters," I said to Nick. "I bet they're beautiful."

"They think they are."

I felt sorry for Nick. I guessed his sisters were as big a problem for him as my brothers were for me.

Suddenly, I felt him stiffen. "Someone's following us," he said.

I turned to look, and I saw a large, dark, yet familiar shape moving up behind us.

"Don't mind me," my brother called out as he passed. "I'm just walking home."

Nick let go of my hand. "Your bodyguard."

"Honestly, Nick, it's just a coincidence."

"Suppose I want to kiss you goodnight," he asked. "Will they turn on a spotlight?"

"Nick," I said, really touched, "do you want to kiss me goodnight?"

The Trouble With Charlie

Jaye Ellen

BANTAM BOOKS
TORONTO · NEW YORK · LONDON · SYDNEY

RL 5, IL age 11 and up

THE TROUBLE WITH CHARLIE
A Bantam Book / October 1982

Cover photo by Michael Bowman.

ISBN 0-553-22957-5

Published simultaneously in the United States and Canada

PRINTED IN THE UNITED STATES OF AMERICA

O   0 9 8 7 6 5 4 3 2

The Trouble
With Charlie

Chapter One

I have often thought of putting a classified ad in the newspaper:

> Free to good home: twin brothers,
> named Adam and Rick, age 17; very
> large, healthy, dark hair, sharp eyes,
> strong-willed, think of themselves as
> watchdogs; all shots and papers; no re-
> funds.

I'm fifteen, and my dating life, which was nothing very remarkable to begin with, almost came to a complete halt because of those brothers. My dad's on an engineering assignment overseas, and after he left, they decided to stand in for him. That was fine when it came to taking out the garbage and fixing the drippy pipe under the sink. But then they started following me around to make sure that I behaved myself.

We live in a small town in Wisconsin called Eagle River. My brothers and I go to the same high school, since there's only one in town. I'm a sophomore. They're both seniors, and to make matters worse, they're big shots on the football team. Our school is small, so it's impossible for me to keep any secrets from them. When word got around school during the fall that my brothers were watching over me, all the guys were afraid to ask me out. There was even a saying going around: Nobody dates Charlie.

That's me—Charlie. And that's partly my brothers' fault, too. I've got a perfectly respectable name—Charlene Carrington. But my father kept calling me Charlie when I was a baby, and my brothers picked it up. To them I was just one of the guys.

Until my first date.

I'm taking an advanced chemistry class, and there's a guy in my class whose name is Frank Hays. He's sixteen, and if you almost close your eyes and stare through your eyelashes at him, he's not bad-looking. One day just before class started, he invited me to a really terrific party. My best friend, Nancy Miller, had been invited two days before; so right away I said yes, I'd love to go.

Then I wondered if I'd sounded too eager, so I started to stammer something about how I'd have to look at my calendar. Only by this time Mrs. Anderson, our chemistry teacher, was trying to call the class to order and saying over and over, "Take out your microscopes, class—your microscopes." So I got mixed up and what I said was that I'd have to look at my cantaloupe.

"Yeah?" Frank said, giving me a funny look and scratching at a pimple on his chin.

If I'm going to die, I thought, it ought to be over somebody other than Frank Hays. So I didn't. I just took a deep breath and said, "I was talking about something else, and it doesn't matter. What time do you want to pick me up?"

"Seven-thirty," he said, and went back to his seat.

I was trying to get my microscope out of the cabinet without banging my knuckles when Frank suddenly appeared at my shoulder. "By the way, where do you live?"

Mrs. Anderson was glaring at us, so I nervously whispered, "In a house."

Well, with a start like that I should have known that nothing about our date was going to go right.

At the dinner table that evening, I told my mother that Frank had invited me to a party. But before she had a chance to answer, Adam put down his fork and said, "You're too young to go."

"It's a birthday party Mike Wilson's parents are giving for him. At least half the people in my class will be there. What's wrong with that?"

"We don't know Mike Wilson," Adam said.

3

"It doesn't make any difference if you know him or not!"

"We don't know Frank Hays either," Rick said.

"Mother!" I complained.

She came through in great style. "I know Mike's mother, and Doris Hays is in my garden club. Help yourself to some string beans, Rick."

Adam frowned. "Are Mike's parents going to be there?"

"Yes, they are," Mom said. "I know all about the party. It's at their house on the lake."

"Okay," he grumbled. "We'll take Charlie and her date and pick them up."

"You will not!" I yelled. "Frank Hays will take me to the party!"

"Is he old enough to drive?" asked Adam.

"Does he have a car?" asked Rick.

"Mother!"

"Rick," Mom said, "that little bit of salad you put on your plate is not going to give you enough vitamins. Have some more, and both of you stop bothering Charlie."

I glared at them from across the table. Although they're twins, no one has trouble telling them apart. That's because they're fraternal and not identical twins. But when it came to interfering with my life and making me miserable, they were exactly the same!

After that, Adam and Rick concentrated on eating dinner, but they kept giving me these corner-of-the-eye looks as though they couldn't believe anyone would ask me out. Oh, for the last year I'd been going to movies and school dances and stuff like that with guys; but it was always with a bunch of kids, and nobody special was involved. This was a real date.

After dinner I called Nancy. "You know that party you're going to at Mike Wilson's lake house?"

"Uh-huh." Nancy was going with Jed Farber, a guy on the football team who in my opinion, isn't very bright but is very good-looking. Nancy is also very good-looking. She has short, dark curly hair and a terrific figure.

"Well, I'm going, too." I said. "With a date."

"Oh, that's great!" Nancy said excitedly. "Who asked you?"

I took a long breath and wished I were saying "Robert Redford." "Frank Hays. He's in my chemistry class."

"Oh." she said. Then, since she is a very optimistic person in addition to being my best friend, she added, "He has great-looking hair."

"Hair?"

"Sure. He's got so much of it, and it's really a very interesting color."

"I guess so," I said.

"He's got a great-looking car, too," she went on. "I heard that as soon as he became sixteen he got a job frying fish at that fast-food place near the mall, and he raised all the money to buy the car by himself."

"How long would he have to fry fish to earn enough to buy a great-looking car?" I asked.

"Well, it's a used car, of course. But let's not talk about his car. Tell me what you're going to wear."

"I don't know," I said. I couldn't concentrate on clothes because the memory of what I had said to Frank was driving me crazy. "Nancy," I went on as if I hadn't heard her, "when Frank asked me to go with him, I said something real stupid."

"That's all right. Everybody says real stupid things when they're nervous."

"Really?"

"Sure. Yesterday in American history Mr. Katz asked Patti to name one of the signers of the Declaration of Independence. But when he called her name, she was thinking about the guy across the aisle, and she said, 'Brian.' Everybody laughed, and Patti looked like she wanted to die."

"At least no one laughed at me."

"What did you say to him?" Nancy asked.

I told her, and she broke up. "You'll probably agonize over it in the middle of the night, but it is funny."

Before I began to feel even worse she changed the subject. "Let's get back to what we're going to wear."

Later, Mom said Mrs. Wilson couldn't possibly be spending as much time getting things ready for the party as Nancy and I were, just thinking about it.

At first I hoped that everyone was going to wear jeans and T-shirts because that's about all I wear. But then the word went around that the girls were going to wear dresses. I have some skirts and blouses but not a dress, so Mom and I went shopping, and I bought one.

"It's a really great color," Nancy said when she saw it. "It matches the blue in your eyes."

Mom looked at me closely. "Your eyes are perfectly beautiful, Charlie. You're becoming a lovely young woman."

I groaned and told Mom to cut it out, but it did make me feel good. A lot of people say I look like Mom. I've seen pictures of her when she was younger, and I think it's true. We have the same color hair, but Mom wears hers very short.

Later, I stared at myself in the bathroom mirror. I sucked in my cheeks so my cheek-bones would look like a model's and held my eyes kind of wide. I thought it looked pretty good if I could just stay that way.

Then I pulled up my hair, which is dark blond and very long, and held it in a neat pile on top of my head. The effect was pretty good. I looked at least eighteen and quite glamorous. After a few minutes, though, my arm began to ache and so did my cheeks, so I shook out my hair and went to finish my homework.

The rest of the week went quickly. We had a nice spell of Indian summer, and the temperature went all the way up to sixty-five degrees. But by Saturday night it was cooler again. It hadn't occurred to me that my brothers would be home when Frank arrived. They usually went out on Saturday nights.

But there they were, both of them, with their broad shoulders and football-player muscles, looking as though they'd squash anyone who came through the front door. And to make things worse, Rick's best friend, Andy Dawson, who lives next door, was there, too. Andy's the same age as Rick and although he's not a football player, he looks like he could be.

"Make them go away, Mom!" I begged.

"We just want to meet your date," Adam said.

"We're trying to be polite," Rick added, with that angelic look he used to put on after he'd pinched me in church.

Andy stared at me. "Gee, you look great, Charlie."

"I think if you boys would—" Mom began, but just then the doorbell rang, and it was too late.

I opened the front door a crack and tried to squeeze through, but Adam, with one hand, pulled it wide.

"Come in, Frank," Adam said, holding out his right hand. He gripped Frank's hand so hard that he made him wince. When Frank leaped inside the house, I knew my brother had pulled him in.

Adam, in his deepest, most solemn voice, introduced Mom, Rick, Andy, and then himself. Those brothers of mine looked down at Frank so intently they could probably see if he'd ever had his tonsils taken out.

"What time will you bring Charlie home?" Adam asked.

"Make it early," Rick said.

"Drive carefully," Adam added.

Andy just grinned.

Mom put an arm around Frank's shoulders and steered him toward the door. "Now, you two have a good time."

Somehow we found ourselves out on the front porch. Frank stared at me, and I tried to think of something clever to say.

"Where's your car?" I asked.

"Right there," he said, pointing. It was the only car on the block.

"We walked toward it. Something had to improve. I tried to think of what Nancy would say. She never has any trouble talking to anyone.

"That's a great-looking car," I said, trying to sound enthusiastic. I'm afraid it came out sounding kind of shocked. That car was really a beat-up hunk of junk.

"Thanks," he said, and he sounded so pleased that I knew it was all right. The door handle came off as he opened the door on my side, but he managed to fasten it on again. "I usually just climb in and out the window," he said. He took a look at me. "But I guess you can't do that. You're wearing a dress."

He looked again. "Hey, you look pretty good, Charlie."

I leaned back against the seat and gave a long sigh of relief. Things were looking up. I tried and tried to think of something else to say. Then I remembered a nursery-school class I helped with one summer. The kids would paint something, and I'd say, "Tell me about your picture," and they'd go on and on about it.

So I said, "Tell me about your car, Frank," and it was good for twenty minutes. By that time we had arrived at the party, and I could be my brilliant self and say, "Oh, look. There's Mike's house."

Surely, I thought, things would get better once we joined the party. They had to.

Chapter Two

Parties in real life are never the way they are on television or in the movies. At those parties people are always saying romantic things and falling in love, and there's a moon lighting everything up and making all the girls look beautiful. But Mr. Wilson had every light in the house turned on, and the most romantic thing anyone said was when Mike told Amelia Krantz she didn't look as fat as she usually did.

There was a guy across the room I hadn't seen before. He was tall and broad-shouldered. He was standing with Amanda Hotchkins, and while I was staring at him, he suddenly looked at me with the most fantastic brown eyes I had ever seen. He smiled. I smiled back. I thought it was kind of dumb to look at someone across the room and feel like this—right out of an old song—but he seemed so terrific.

"Who is that?" I whispered to Nancy.

"Mark Potter," she said when she saw who I was looking at. "He and his family just moved here this fall from Seattle, Washington. He's in my geometry class, and I think he's kind of shy."

Whenever I got the chance I looked over at Mark, and a couple of times I caught him looking at me. Once I even got close enough to him to say hi, and he said hi, but that's absolutely all that happened. Amanda wouldn't leave him alone for a minute. Besides, I couldn't think of anything to talk about. I never used to have this problem. Why had it suddenly become so hard to talk to guys?

I guess Mrs. Wilson thought the party wasn't lively enough because Mike had put on some records and she kept going around asking, "Wouldn't anyone like to dance?" She couldn't seem to realize that we don't dance much at parties. Most of my friends just sit around, talking, listening to records, and eating.

Mrs. Wilson was beginning to look desperate, and her frantic glance landed on me. "Charlie! Why don't you sing for us? Your mother tells me you have a lovely voice."

"That's right," Nancy said. She gave me a little shove forward.

I stepped back, mashing someone's toes. "Not here. Not now," I mumbled. "I need some music to sing with."

"She sings with records," Nancy said. "Do you have any Barbra Streisand records?"

"Nancy," I muttered, "you're supposed to be my friend. No one wants to hear me sing."

"Of course we do," Mrs. Wilson insisted putting on a record.

Nobody but Nancy knows that my dream is to be as famous as Barbra Streisand. Oh well, I thought, if I'm going to be a star someday, I may as well start singing in front of an audience.

Mrs. Wilson found an old Streisand record, but I know the words to everything she's ever recorded, so I stood by the stereo and belted out a song, right along with her. Some of the kids even listened to me. I relaxed and kind of enjoyed myself, but I didn't look in Mark's direction. I had stared right into his eyes when I started to sing, and my knees got wobbly, so I quickly looked away.

While I was singing, Dolores, the head cheerleader at school, slipped out to the back porch with Hank, her date. Some of the girls looked at each other and grinned. Mr. and Mrs. Wilson, who were politely looking at me, didn't even notice.

But in a few minutes we heard a crash and a yell. Dolores had sat on the railing, which had given way, and she had landed in a rosebush. Mrs. Wilson had to take her into the bedroom and pick out thorns with a tweezers. Meanwhile, Mr. Wilson stood next to the buffet table with his arms folded, watching to make sure that no one tried to slip out of the house again.

"This is a really great party," Nancy said. She started doing a dance step that she made up. That got some of the kids interested, and they got up and started dancing. Frank even asked me to dance.

I don't know what kind of step we were doing, but every now and then he'd kick sideways. A couple of times I got it in the ankle, and I heard Janie yell "Ouch!" so I'm sure I wasn't the only victim. I became very cautious. When I thought Frank's foot was coming my way, I jumped to the side.

Pretty soon Mrs. Wilson came back with Dolores, who was trying not to walk funny, and said we should all start for home so our parents wouldn't worry. Everybody said goodbye, and thanked Mike for the party.

When we got into Frank's car, he said, "Some party. It's only ten-thirty."

"We could get something to eat," I suggested.

He looked kind of miserable. "I ate too much already."

He started the car, and as he drove I tried to think of something to say. Nothing sounded right.

All of a sudden Frank turned the car onto a narrow dirt road.

"Where are you going?" I asked. I sat up straight and tried to keep the sun visor from flopping up and down as we bounced over the potholes.

"I took this road once before," he said. "It's a shortcut."

There were big, open fields on both sides of the road and one farmhouse down the way, but otherwise there were no signs of civilization. Frank slowed down the car and steered it toward the side of the road.

"Car trouble," he said. He smiled as he looked at me.

I had my mouth open to say something when there was a lurch and a bump that rattled my teeth. We came to a stop, and the car tilted way down on the front right side.

"Oh, no!" Frank yelled.

He scrambled out of the window on his side and ran around to the front of the car. "The wheel came off!"

"Oh-oh," I said, leaning out of my window. "Is the axle damaged?"

I climbed out of the car through the window. No point in making him more unhappy by handing him the door handle.

"Have you got a flashlight?" I asked. "A jack? A wrench?"

"No. Three hundred dollars only goes so far."

"There's a house over there," I said. "We can walk to it and ask if we can use the telephone. Maybe my brothers can come and get us." There were no lights on in the house, and I hated to wake the people up, but I didn't know what else to do.

Frank looked sick. "I'd better call my father."

Luckily there was a bright moon so we could see where we were walking. We found a long driveway leading to the farmhouse. It was a ratty-looking place, with junk rusting in the front yard. As we got closer I could see that the house was abandoned. Its doors were gone and the windows broken.

"I guess we'll have to wait for a car to come along," I said.

"Not many cars come this way. It's a dead-end road."

"I thought you said it was a shortcut."

"Yeah, Well, I thought—"

"That was a dumb trick," I snapped, wishing I could punch him out. I sat down on the porch steps.

Frank sat beside me. "It was dumb, you're right. Don't be mad at me, Charlie. It's just that we didn't have to be home for a while, and so I hoped. . . ."

All of a sudden, Frank put his arms around me and tried to nuzzle my neck. I hadn't expected this, and for a second I froze on the spot. Then I pushed him away and jumped up.

"Frank Hays! What do you think you're doing?"

Frank looked up at me, a startled expression on his face. He didn't say anything, and I was getting annoyed.

"You got us into this mess," I said, "so you'd better figure out a way to get us out of it. How are we going to get home now?"

Frank looked embarrassed. He got up and went to the far end of the bottom step. Then he sat down again and put his head in his hands. "I don't know what to do next," he whined.

"We can either walk back to the highway where we can hitch a ride to town, or we can sit here and wait for someone to come and find us," I said.

Frank groaned. It was obvious that he couldn't make a decision. "It's a long way back to the highway," he said finally.

I looked around. We were in the middle of nowhere, and except for the light of the moon, it was pretty dark. The thought of spending the rest of the night outside, or in the car, made me shiver. I had worn a light jacket, and it was a cool night. We could go in the house, but without a flashlight there was no telling what we might bump into.

Frank and I didn't speak for several minutes. I was thinking over all our options. Finally I decided that we should try to get help.

"Come on, Frank," I said. "Let's walk back to the highway. Our families will be frantic if we don't get home soon."

Reluctantly, Frank agreed and followed me back to the dirt road. He looked wistfully at his car as we passed it. "Don't worry," I told him. "We'll call a tow truck when we get back to town."

Frank was right about one thing. It was a long walk back to the highway. It took us over an hour, and my feet were killing me by the time we reached it.

Although the highway is a major interstate, there wasn't much traffic that night. We waved at every car that passed by, but they were moving pretty fast. The drivers either didn't see us or simply chose not to stop. After fifteen minutes, a car finally pulled over. Frank and I looked at each other. *Just our luck*, I thought. It was a police car.

The officer stepped out and approached us. "Hitchhiking is illegal on state highways," he said sternly. "I'll have to give you kids tickets."

"Wait a minute, officer!" I said.

"A wheel came off my car," Frank broke in nervously. "It's parked down that dirt road a few miles. We were just trying to get a ride back to town so we could call our parents and a tow truck."

The officer studied us for a moment and then said, "OK. Climb in the backseat. I'll radio for a tow truck and then take you kids back to the station. You can call your parents from there."

Can you imagine calling home and telling your family you're at the police station? As soon as Mom found out that I was all right, she calmed down and said not to worry about a thing. Adam had just arrived home, and the two of them would come and get me.

When they walked into the police station, Mom gave me a big hug and smiled and said it was no one's fault and if that was the worst thing that ever happened to me, she'd be glad. But Adam kept scowling at Frank.

"Can't you trust me, Adam?" I cried.

"Of course he can," Mom said. "And he can trust Frank, too."

When she said that, Frank immediately looked guilty, which was a mistake, because Adam glared down at him. "Nothing like this had better happen again!"

"Believe me, it won't!" I said.

At the time I meant it. How was I to know about the trouble ahead?

Chapter Three

F_{rank} Hays didn't ask me out again, which was all right with me. Nancy said Frank was immature, and I agreed. "Forget this date," she told me. "Wipe it out of your mind. The next date is going to be better."

"Anything would be better," I said.

Two days later, during lunch period, Nancy banged her cafeteria tray on the table next to my tray and climbed over the bench to sit beside me. "I heard from Jed that somebody at the party thinks you're fantastic and is going to ask you out."

Immediately I thought of Mark Potter. I had just taken a bite of tuna salad, and I was so excited I almost choked. "Who?" I asked.

"Steve," she said, banging on my back.

Finally I caught my breath, put down my fork and stared at her. "Steve Kemp?"

"That's right," she said with the kind of enthusiasm that ought to be saved for Christmas and birthdays.

"I've known Steve Kemp since kindergarten," I mumbled.

"Don't let that influence you. Everybody looks awful while they're growing up, but you must have noticed that Steve has changed a lot. He has a really great bone structure. You just haven't studied his face closely."

Just as we finished our lunches, Steve and Jed came over to the table, put their trays down, and sat on the bench across from us. I took a long, hard look at Steve, trying to appreciate his bone structure. However, he had a huge wad of adhesive tape over his nose, so it was hard to tell if Nancy was right.

"Hi, Charlie," he said, humming through his nose as he talked.

"Steve broke his nose in football practice yesterday," Jed explained.

"I'm sorry," I said.

"Forget it." Steve shrugged. "I made a dumb mistake, and I don't want to think about it."

I tried not to stare at his nose, but it wasn't easy. I looked at his chin and then into his eyes. They were a nice shade of green, but they weren't as fascinating as that bandage, and my glance kept zapping toward it as though it were a magnet.

Nancy suddenly got up from the table and grabbed her tray. "Come on, Jed."

"Where?" Jed asked. "I haven't finished my lunch!"

Nancy made a face at him. "We've got to see somebody."

"Who?"

"Oh, never mind!" she said. "Jed, will you just get up from there and come with me!"

Jed looked at us and shrugged as he untangled his legs from the bench. "See you guys later." He picked up his tray and left.

After they had gone, Steve said, "I saw you at Mike's party. You stepped on my foot."

"I'm sorry."

"I never heard you sing before. It was pretty good. You sounded sort of like Barbra Streisand, only a lot louder."

"Thanks."

"There's a Burt Reynolds movie starting on Friday. Would you like to go with me?"

"Sure. I'd really like that."

"Where do you live?"

This time my mind was razor sharp. I gave him my address.

Once that was done there didn't seem to be anything more to say. Steve was still finishing his lunch, so I clutched the edge of my tray and stumbled to my feet. "I've got to get some stuff out of my bell before the locker rings." I muttered.

"I'll pick you up at seven," Steve said.

"Great," I answered. I couldn't get out of there fast enough.

That evening I made the mistake of telling Mom about my date with Steve Kemp while Rick and Adam were in the room.

"What's the rating on the movie you're going to?" Adam wanted to know.

"It better not be at a drive-in," Rick said.

"Mother!" I shouted.

"Adam," she said, "please don't pester Charlie."

"We just want to know something about her date," Rick said.

"I don't think Charlie should see the movie unless we think it's all right," Adam added.

"Why can't you go to a Walt Disney movie?" Rick teased me.

I glared at them. "It isn't fair! When either of you go out and Mom asks where you're going, you just mumble something or you say, 'I don't know,' or 'out with the guys,' or some dumb thing like that."

"That's different," Rick said.

"Why is it different? Women are supposed to have equal rights, aren't they?"

"It's debatable," Adam said.

"Mother!"

Mom broke in. "Charlie has a good point. From now on I'm going to insist on getting a little more information from both of you when you go out."

Good old Mom. My brothers changed the subject in a hurry.

I honestly thought this time would be different, but just before Steve was supposed to arrive, Adam and Rick came downstairs, ready to meet him.

"What are you doing here?" I said.

"Dad would be here to greet your date," Adam said, "so it's only right that we take his place. If someone's going to take out our kid sister, we'd like to check him out."

"But you already know Steve from school!" I said, trying to control my temper. "He's even on the football team!"

"Yeah, but that's different," said Rick. "If he's out with you, we want to make sure he behaves himself."

"It's none of your business!" I shouted. "Mother!"

She was coming into the living room when the doorbell rang. I made a dash for the door, but Adam got to it first and opened it wide. Steve just stood on the porch staring up at Adam.

Adam clamped a hand on Steve's shoulder and propelled him into the room. Everyone said hello, and mother introduced herself.

"That's too bad about your nose," Rick said.

"Don't talk about it," I said, gritting my teeth.

"Sure looks terrible," Rick added.

"Be quiet!" I demanded. "Steve doesn't want to talk about it!"

"I don't blame him," Adam said.

Mother stepped in. "You two run along and enjoy your movie," she said.

"Thanks," Steve mumbled.

We managed to get out of the house, but that was just the first step. Now I had to think of something to say.

I was seated in the car, and we were on our way downtown, when I realized with an enormous sense of relief that I could repeat my conversational success of last week. "Tell me about your car."

"It's not mine," Steve said. "It's my father's."

"Oh." I wondered what to say next. "It's a nice car, isn't it?"

"Sure."

"It has a radio and everything."

"Most cars do."

"I guess we'll see a lot of cars tonight," I said.

Steve looked at me oddly.

"I mean in the movie. I mean in Burt Reynolds movies there are usually a lot of car chases and car crashes and all that. That's what I mean. I mean I was just thinking about the movie."

"Yeah." Steve looked at me again. The white

bandage on his nose seemed even bigger in the dark. "Don't you like Burt Reynolds?"

"Of course," I said quickly. "I wasn't objecting to the car chases. They're really exciting. I love the way Burt Reynolds always wins."

I decided that movies are great for dates. You can just watch, and you don't have to say anything at all. Steve got us a giant-size box of popcorn, Cokes, and a couple of candy bars, and we just settled back and watched the movie.

After we ate everything, Steve reached for my hand. I felt very self-conscious, and I forgot about the movie. Steve was holding my hand! Unfortunately, our hands sort of stuck together and we sweated a lot. I didn't know whether I should let go of his hand or not. I wondered if he was thinking the same thing.

I was sorry when the movie was over because then I had to try to think of something to talk about. Then I got the brilliant idea of talking about the movie.

So that's what I did until I noticed we were driving in the wrong direction. "Where are we going?"

"To get something to eat," he said. "It's early and there's this place my older brother talks about all the time. He says they've got the best hamburgers in town."

I guess it's true what they say about feeling closer to someone who's in the same boat as you. I liked Steve a lot better when I learned he had an older brother, too.

"What's the name of this hamburger place?" I asked.

"The Moose Head."

I tried to think of something clever to say but couldn't.

We made a turn and found ourselves on a crummy-looking street. Even Steve seemed a little worried. "My brother recommended it, so it must be OK."

At the end of the block was a building with a big moose head painted on the front. The paint was peeling, and it made the moose look as if it had a skin disease. Steve parked right in front, turned off the ignition, and just sat there staring at the place.

"I wonder what it's like inside," he said.

I jumped out of the car and tried to sound enthusiastic. "Let's find out!"

Chapter Four

As soon as we went inside, I realized I might have made a mistake. It was kind of dim. Well, it was a lot dim. All I could see was a small ring of light that covered a tiny stage and three musicians who looked as seedy as the moose outside. Steve, walking closely behind, bumped into me. I fell over a chair, with someone in it, so I ended up in his lap.

A large hand grabbed my arm and pulled me to my feet. "If you've already had too much to drink, don't come in here!" the man growled in my ear.

"I haven't had anything to drink," I said. "I can't see where I'm going. It's dark in here."

"Come on," he said. "I'll find you a table."

By the time we were seated, the musicians had stopped playing. The lights got a little brighter, so we could see around the room. It was full of guys making a lot of noise, and, I judged from the number of mugs on the table, drinking a lot of beer.

A man with a dirty apron over his jeans came over and said, "You're too young to drink."

"I just want a Coke," I said. "And a hamburger."

"Make that two hamburgers," Steve added.

The waiter stared at Steve's nose. "Ain't you the one who started that fight in here last week?"

Steve shook his head. "Not me."

The waiter left, and I said, "Steve, does your brother look like you? Could he have been in the fight?"

"He wasn't here last week. He has mono."

I got this horrible feeling that he must have caught it here, but I tried to think of something else to keep the conversation sparkling.

"If the musicians come back, maybe we can dance," I said.

"There's no place to dance."

"Oh."

Fortunately, in a few minutes the hamburgers came. They were at least three inches high, and Steve's brother was right. They were terrific hamburgers.

The musicians came back and started playing. They were good, and I was enjoying the music when a shape loomed up in the dark and shoved something into Steve's hand. "Here's your check," the waiter said. He stood there with his hand out.

"It's too dark. I can't read it," Steve said.

So the man told him, and we both gasped. "Are you sure that's right?" Steve asked. "I didn't think anybody charged that much for hamburgers!"

"There's a cover charge because of the music," he said. "Pay up."

Steve turned to me. "Could I borrow five dollars? I haven't got enough money with me."

"All I've got is a couple of quarters in case I have to call home."

"Listen, fella," the waiter said, leaning toward Steve, "just pay the bill."

Steve and I looked at each other. Then Steve turned back to the waiter.

"I'm sorry, sir," he said. "But I'll have to go home first and get some more money. We'll be back in just ten minutes, I promise."

"What?" the waiter bellowed. "You really believe I'm gonna let you out of here without paying your bill? How do I know if I'll ever see you again? I wasn't born yesterday, you know. That's an old trick. And besides, whenever customers leave without paying the check, the manager makes the waiter who took care of them pay the bill."

"But it's not a trick!" I shouted back. "We intend to pay the bill. We just didn't bring enough money with us, that's all. Nobody else in town charges that much for a couple of hamburgers."

"Oh, yeah? Well, you should have looked at the price before you ordered 'em. Joe! Come on over here!" He signaled to a man in a blue suit, who I figured was the manager.

"What's the problem?" he asked.

"Got a couple of kids here who are trying to skip out without paying the bill," said the waiter.

"We are not trying to skip out!" protested Steve. "We just have to go home and get some more money before—"

"Shut up!" Joe snapped. He looked even meaner than the waiter. "We know how to handle kids like you. Call the police!"

In a flash, Steve was on his feet. "Wait! Don't call the police! First, let me call my brother. He'll bring some cash over right away, and we'll stay here until he arrives.

Joe and the waiter exchanged glances. "Well, OK," Joe said. "But you'd better have change for the pay phone. It's over there." He indicated the rear of the restaurant, then turned back to the waiter. "Don't let them out of your sight until the check is paid," he snarled.

"Right," said the waiter, glaring at me as Steve disappeared to make the call. A few minutes later, Steve returned, looking upset.

"There's no answer. What do we do now?"

"I thought for a moment. "Well," I said, reluctantly, "it looks like I'm going to have to call Rick and Adam. I don't want to do that, but there's no other way we're going to get out of here without going to the police station. I'd better warn you, though. They're not going to like the fact that I'm in a place like this, and they might take it out on you."

Steve groaned. "Swell," he mumbled, "let's get it over with."

I walked back to the pay phone and dialed my number. Rick answered. Quickly, I explained the situation.

"What restaurant?"

When I told him it was called the Moose Head, he exploded on the other end of the phone. "What are you doing in a dive like that, Charlie? That happens to be just about the crumbiest restaurant in town. There are fights in there all the time!"

"Well, they have good hamburgers," I explained weakly.

Rick and Adam were there in less than fifteen minutes. They must have driven like crazy to have made it that fast. Steve turned pale when they entered the restaurant.

I waved to them, and they hurried over to our table. So did the waiter. He stood nearby, ready to take the money.

"Hi, Rick, hi, Adam!" I said, trying to sound cheerful. "I'm sorry you had to come all the way over here." I hoped that they could see a little humor in the situation.

Rick glanced around the room. He shook

his head. "This place is even worse than I thought," he muttered. "What a dive!"

Adam glared down at Steve and took out his wallet. "How much do you need to cover the check?"

Steve cleared his throat nervously. "Five dollars. I'll pay you back." He took the money Adam handed him.

Steve paid the check and we got up to leave. At that moment, Joe saw us and came running over. "Don't come back," he warned us, "unless you can afford to eat here. This ain't no fast food place!"

We hurried outside. I didn't know quite what to expect from Rick and Adam, but I could feel myself getting defensive.

"I'll take Charlie home," Steve said.

"We'll take her home," Adam told him.

"No you won't," I said angrily.

"Why'd you take her to a place like this?" Rick asked Steve.

"My brother said they make good hamburgers," Steve said. He was right, but it sure sounded dumb.

"We don't want you to take her here again," Adam said.

"Don't worry, I won't!" It was pretty obvious that Steve wasn't going to take me *anywhere* again.

"After this," Adam said to Rick, "We'll have to supervise Charlie more closely."

"We owe it to Dad," Rick agreed.

"Now wait a minute!" I told them. "I am not going to spend my dating life being followed around by you!"

I turned to Steve. "I'm sorry. Please take me home."

At our front door Steve said a quick good night, keeping about five feet between us. His eyes darted from side to side as though he were afraid my brothers would suddenly jump out of the bushes.

I went upstairs and woke up Mom. When she turned on the table lamp, I could see a stack of Dad's letters next to it. We all miss Dad and I know it must be extra hard for Mom while he's working overseas. She and Dad really love each other a lot.

I told her about my date. She looked as if she were trying hard not to smile. "It wasn't funny, Mom!" But then I had to smile, too, and it didn't seem to be such a calamity.

I sat on the edge of the bed. "Mom, I thought dating was going to be so terrific."

"It is," she assured me, "when you're with a boy you like."

"I don't know any boys I like." And then I thought about Mark Potter and knew I could learn to like him in a hurry.

"Besides," I said, "there's something wrong with me. I don't know what to say to guys."

"You talk to your brothers."

"That's different."

"Not really. The point I'm trying to make is

that you're relaxed with your brothers, so it's easy to talk to them. When you're with a date, all you have to do is be yourself and you'll find that the conversation will come naturally."

She smiled. "And there's nothing wrong with you. Most girls who are beginning to date feel just the way you do."

"So what's the secret? What can I do about it?"

"Charlie," Mom said, "when you meet a boy you really like as a person and you start thinking of him as a person and not as a 'date,' you'll find you can enjoy talking to him."

I sat there thinking about some of the girls I know who always seem relaxed with guys. I wondered if Mom was right. "Any more questions, Charlie?"

"Yes. What do you do if a boy you like doesn't ask you out?"

"Let him know that you find him interesting," she said.

"I can't do that!" I said. Then I told her all about Mark Potter and how much I wanted him to ask me out.

"Then why don't *you* ask *him* out?"

I groaned. "Mom! I couldn't!" I slid off the bed and picked up my shoes. Nancy was the one I needed to talk to. But she was out with Jed so I'd have to wait to call her.

When I did speak to Nancy, she said, "Maybe I could tell Jed you like Mark, and he could pass the word along."

"That's too embarrassing." Then I added, "Nancy, I really don't think dating is as terrific as we thought it would be."

"Don't worry, Charlie," she reassured me. "When you start at the bottom, things are bound to get better."

I clung to that thought until my disastrous date with Carl Anderson.

Chapter Five

Somebody in the PTA got the bright idea of giving a square dance for our grade. It was probably Mrs. Hotchkins, who is always coming up with new ideas. This time she made a big mistake.

In the first place none of us know how to square dance. Mrs. Hotchkins said it would be fun to learn and that there would be a genuine square-dance caller to teach us. We all knew the caller would turn out to be Mr. Hotchkins because he's been everything for the PTA, including Santa Claus at Christmas time.

In the second place she announced that this would be a dance to which the girls would invite the boys.

"I can't do it," I told Nancy when we met in

front of school at the end of the day. "I don't even know who to invite."

"Sure you do," Nancy said. She was so excited she dropped her books all over the sidewalk. We were both picking them up when she added, "You can ask Mark Potter."

The idea scared me to death. As I handed her her books, I said, "You're crazy," I told her. "He doesn't even know who I am. All we ever said to each other was hi."

"What difference does that make?"

"It makes a big difference to me. I have to get to know him first."

"Get to know him at the dance."

"He'd turn me down if I asked him."

"How do you know if you don't try?"

"He's probably still dating Amanda."

"You act like they're engaged. I bet he's tired of her by this time."

I thought about that for a minute. "You really think I should ask him?"

"Yes," Nancy said. She moved close and nudged me. "He's coming this way, and no one's with him. Now's your chance."

I was terrified. My heart began to pound, and I was sure everyone around could hear it.

"Go on," Nancy was whispering. "Now!"

He was almost beside me. I managed to open my mouth. "Hi, Mark," I said.

He stopped and smiled at Nancy and me. "Hi," he said.

"Hi," I said again, hoping he couldn't see that I was trembling.

"Oh! I forgot something in my locker," Nancy said, moving away at the nearest thing to a run.

"I haven't had a chance to talk to you since the party at Mike's house," Mark said.

"Speaking of parties." I was so nervous I could hardly talk. "Have you heard about the square dance the PTA is giving for our class?"

"That's all Mrs. Hotchkins talks about," he said.

"Mrs. Hotchkins? Oh. You're probably going with Amanda." My mouth was dry. I shouldn't have said that. But I knew it must be true.

He nodded. "You'll be there, won't you?"

"Sure," I managed to say.

I think he said goodbye before he walked on. Actually I'm not sure what he said. I was just thankful that I hadn't mortified myself by inviting him to that dance.

As soon as he had reached the corner, Nancy came racing over to me. "Well? Well? What happened?" she asked, grabbing my arm.

"Nothing," I said. "He's going to the dance with Amanda." I felt like crying.

"Rats!" Nancy exclaimed. Then her optimism took over. "But he talked to you for a while. That's something. What did he say?"

"He asked if I'd be at the dance."

"You see!" Nancy broke into a big smile. "He's interested in you. That's a good start."

"You're hopeless," I told her, even though she did make me feel a little better about the whole thing.

"And the nice part about it is that you'll be dancing with him anyway, because in square dances you dance with everybody."

"You're right," I said, feeling a little better.

"Just think. For a second or two, you'll be in his arms."

I was feeling so good by the time we reached the corner that when we bumped into Carl Anderson I recklessly said, "Carl, how would you like to go to the square dance with me?"

I've known Carl since he used to kick my shins under the table during library period in fourth grade. As it happens he turned into kind of a nice person after he got over his kicking phase. He'd grown tall and thin and was almost good-looking.

"Huh?" Carl said. "You want me to be your date, Charlie?"

All I could do was nod. Why had I asked Carl? What in the world could we talk about except how it felt to be kicked in the shins?

Anyway, Carl looked pleased. "OK," he said. Then he added, "I'd walk you home, except I'm late for my clarinet lesson."

So I smiled and waved, and Nancy and I crossed the street.

"Hmmm," Nancy said. "You really surprised me, but he's an interesting choice. Carl's highly thought of in the marching band."

"Why in the world did I ask Carl? I don't think I've even spoken to him more than five or six times since fourth grade. And what I said to him then wasn't very nice."

"That doesn't matter. The point," Nancy reminded me, "is to get to the party so you can dance with Mark Potter. And now you're on your way!"

I tried not to think about how terrible it would be to pick Carl up because he wasn't old enough to drive. Of course I knew who would be our pilot and co-pilot. Adam and Rick, the super pests.

The party was on a Friday night, and as I figured, Rick and Adam insisted on driving us. It was being held in the school gym, and fortunately the school was just a short drive from Carl's house. Somehow I managed to live through that part of it, with both of them keeping an eye on us—Adam through the rear-view mirror and Rick by simply turning around and staring at us. At least Rick kept up the conversation with Carl.

Adam parked the car, and he and Rick got out. "We'll see you to the door," Adam said.

I was so mad I just turned, grabbed Carl's hand, and dragged him into the gym. My brothers followed closely behind.

Mrs. Hotchkins and her committee had gone all out in decorating the gym. There were several bales of hay around the room and a big table with punch and sandwiches. Some of the

43

kids were sitting on the bales of hay and some were standing around.

As soon as we entered the gym, Mrs. Hotchkins spied my brothers and came running over.

"Thank heavens!" she said, grabbing on to Rick and Adam. "Two big, strong boys. Just what I need! Would you be so kind as to bring in some more bales of hay from the truck out back? We'll need them for extra seating. A couple of seniors who were supposed to help me never showed up, and I'm a little behind. So be good boys and come along. . . ."

Before Rick and Adam could protest, Mrs. Hotchkins pulled them through the crowd to the back door of the gym.

"Swell," I said to Carl. "Now they'll probably stay here for the whole party. Carl?"

I looked around, but Carl was gone. He was over at the table, talking to some of his friends. Suddenly Nancy appeared at my side.

"You look terrific!" she whispered. "I love your denim skirt. Mark is going to think you're gorgeous."

"Would you believe my brothers are staying to help Mrs. Hotchkins?" I was still sputtering as I looked around the room, trying to find Mark.

Before Nancy could say any more, Mrs. Hotchkins was talking over the microphone, her voice bright and eager. "It's time for the square dancing to begin. And here's our square-dance caller!"

Sure enough, Mr. Hotchkins came out in overalls and a plaid shirt. He was wearing a red kerchief around his neck and a straw hat on his head. He looked miserable, probably because Mrs. Hotchkins was the only one applauding. But he took the mike and tried to sound jovial, telling us to form double circles—boys on the outside and girls on the inside.

"Don't worry about your brothers," Nancy said. "In a few minutes you'll be dancing with Mark!"

I wished she hadn't said that, because just then Mark looked at me. As our eyes met, I could feel my face turning red.

Mrs. Hotchkins put on a record. Mr. Hotchkins had the circles move in opposite directions in time to the music, so I kept passing Mark, and each time I did I gave him a big smile. Mark smiled back, and in a few minutes I forgot about Adam and Rick.

But Carl began to look strange. His eyes got red, as though he'd been crying. And the next time I passed him his eyes looked puffy. And the time after that it was hard to see his eyes because he had them squeezed shut and was blowing his nose.

"Now link arms with the people you're passing," Mr. Hotchkins called. "In and out and in and out."

I had my eyes on Mark. He was moving closer and closer to me. He was smiling at me! In just a few seconds he'd take my arm! My knees felt wobbly, and it was hard to breathe.

Suddenly someone said loudly, "Stop the music!" It was Adam.

"What's the matter?" Mrs. Hotchkins asked. She turned off the record. "What's happening over there?"

Adam took Carl's arm and pulled him out of the circle. By this time he was wheezing. "Something's the matter with Carl," Adam said.

"I'm all right," he said. "It's just my allergies."

"My goodness," Mrs. Hotchkins said. "Carl looks terrible. This could be serious."

Adam turned to Mrs. Hotchkins. "We'll take them home."

"*Them?*" I blurted out.

"Of course," Adam said to me in a low voice. "Your date is ill. You can't just send him home and stay."

"I don't want to go home," Carl insisted as Adam and Rick propelled him toward the door.

Mrs. Hotchkins turned the music back on, and everyone began circling again. I didn't even look back. I just followed Carl and my brothers out of the gym.

Carl sulked in the backseat. I didn't know whether to feel sorrier for him or for myself. In fact, I felt miserable enough to cover both of us.

He didn't say anything until we pulled up in front of his house. "I've heard about how bossy your brothers are," he mumbled, staring at me from his puffy red eyes. "It's true!"

As he went through his front door and Adam steered the car away from the curb I said, "That's the end of Carl."

"Don't be dumb," Rick said. "He'll be all right once he takes his allergy pills."

"That's not what I meant." I was really angry. "Why do you always have to tell my dates what to do?"

"We have to try to do what Dad would do if he were here," Adam answered.

"Listen to me," I shouted. "Don't try to be Dad. Stay out of my dating life! I mean it!"

But they began talking about football scores and ignored me.

When we got home, I was the first one inside the house, and I slammed the front door behind me. "Mom!" I yelled, before I remembered that she had gone out to dinner with some friends. I just stood there in the middle of the living room wondering what I was going to do and hoping I wouldn't start to cry.

In a few minutes the front door opened, and Adam and Rick came in. Right behind them was Andy.

"I saw you come home," Andy said. "That was a short party."

"Her date got sick," Adam said. "We had to take him home."

"Tough luck," Andy said.

"Naw," Rick said. "We didn't want to stick around there anyway."

"I didn't mean for you," Andy said. "I meant for Charlie."

He looked at me as though he really was sorry. For a guy who has spent most of his life either ignoring me or pulling my hair, that was an improvement.

"The evening is young," Rick said. "You guys want to take in a movie?"

"Why not?" Adam said.

"You want to come, too, Charlie?" Andy asked.

My brothers, who were already heading toward the door, stopped and stared at him.

"Well, Charlie's here, too," Andy pointed out.

"She wouldn't want to go with us, anyway," Adam said.

I held my chin high and spoke slowly and disdainfully, hoping Rick and Adam would wilt under my total disgust. "Right," I said. "I would not dream of going anywhere with either of you. Never. Not any time in my whole life."

"See, I told you she'd say no," Adam said.

"OK," Andy said. "It's just that Charlie looks terrific all dressed up like that. If she stays home alone it will all go to waste."

"Come on, let's go," Rick said.

Before I could even think up a rejoinder, they were outside, and the door was firmly shut. And there I was, all alone in the house with no one to talk to. I couldn't call Nancy because she was still at the party. Maybe I should get a diary, I thought. And then I remembered the time Aunt Gladys gave me one for my thirteenth birthday and I started writing down my thoughts. I was only two weeks into it when Rick got it out of my secret hiding place and read it. He even quoted from it at the dinner table. Dad really scolded him, but that didn't mean Rick wouldn't do it again if he had the chance.

Not knowing what else to do, I turned on the television and got a commercial for denture cream. I'd be old enough for dentures before my dating life improved, at the rate it was going. Oh, well, if there wasn't anything else to do, for a little while I could enjoy feeling sorry for myself.

Life picked up considerably the next morning when Nancy phoned to tell me that nobody had had a very good time at the dance.

"Jed told me something very, very interesting," Nancy continued, sounding mysterious.

"What?"

"Jack Byars told Jed he likes you."

"Who's Jack Byars?"

"That guy who transferred here last month from Ohio. You know."

"No, I don't know."

"He's in your English class."

"Where does he sit?"

"I don't know. I'm not there."

"Is he good-looking?"

"Dark hair, blue eyes."

"How come I haven't noticed him? Is he tall?"

"Not terribly tall."

I began to get suspicious. "Nancy," I said. "Is this Jack Byars short? Is he shorter than I am?"

"I don't know why you'd care how tall he is," she answered. "Height isn't as important as other things."

I sighed. "What other things?"

"Well," she said, "word gets around. Jed said that a lot of guys don't want to date you because your brothers scare them."

All I could do was groan.

"So the point is to get out and have fun and let everyone know that your brothers aren't going to be a problem."

I thought about that for a moment and shifted the telephone receiver to my other ear. "I guess height isn't everything."

"That's the best way to look at it," Nancy said. "I'll tell Jed to tell Jack that you're interested."

Chapter Six

I was very curious about Jack by the time I got to my English class on Monday. Mrs. Jensen never calls roll out loud. She just lets her eyes skim up and down the rows while she mumbles names under her breath. My desk was near the middle of the room, so I decided this Jack must sit behind me somewhere, and I kept sneaking quick looks around, which didn't help at all because they were too quick. But I didn't want Mrs. Jensen to catch me.

The minute the bell rang, however, this guy appeared at my side, standing so close I had to stare up at him. "Hi," he said. "I'm Jack Byars."

"Hi," I said. It was hard to tell how tall he was from where I sat, so I stood up in order to find out. To my surprise, I looked down, down,

down at him. I guess Jack Byars came about up to my ear, and I had the feeling I should bend over and pat him on the head.

"Somebody told me you sing like Barbra Streisand," he said. "That's pretty good. I do a movie star imitation, too. Bet you can't guess who."

I was tempted to say Mickey Rooney, but instead I said, "Who?"

"Humphrey Bogart," he answered. Then he curled his lower lip and mumbled something.

"What did you say?"

"I said, 'Here's lookin' at you, kid.' That was my Bogart impersonation."

"Oh. That was pretty good," I said.

"The art cinema is showing an old Bogart movie Friday night," he said. "Would you like to go with me?"

"OK." I gave him my phone number, although I wasn't wildly enthusiastic.

After school I said to Nancy, "Why am I doing this?"

"To have a date."

"Dating doesn't seem to be that great."

"It will be," Nancy promised, "as soon as you get past the rough spots."

"When will that be?"

"I'm not sure," she said. "I think you'll know when it happens."

"At least the movie's supposed to be good," I said.

Nancy beamed at me. "Look at it this way. Jack is young. He'll grow."

I found out later that Adam had plans to go to the same Bogart movie that night, with a date. For once, he didn't ask to drive us. I was glad about that, but I didn't want to tell Jack that my brother would be there. After all, there was already a lot of talk about my brothers following me around and scaring all my dates. This time, however, it would be pure coincidence, and I didn't want to give Jack the wrong impression.

Jack's mother offered to drive us, and they arrived a little early. Fortunately, Rick and Adam were still upstairs so we escaped without any hassle. In spite of having to look down on Jack, things were looking up.

When Jack's mother dropped us off at the art cinema, we told her we would call her when we were ready to go home. The art cinema is the oldest theater in town. When we sat down, I noticed the curtain was torn and patched in several places and that a lot of bulbs were missing from the huge crystal chandelier overhead. Our seats were covered with velvet and were very rickety. Every time Jack leaned toward me to say something, his chair creaked.

I didn't see Adam and his date come in, but then I wasn't really looking for them, and we were down in front, anyway. The movie was *Casablanca*, and I got interested in it right away. It had to do with the Second World War, and Ingrid Bergman was trying to help her husband escape from the Nazis. Jack's chair squeaked as he moved closer to me and took my hand. About the time Ingrid Bergman told the piano player to play the love song, Jack put his arm around me.

The story flashed back to Paris, where Bergman was saying goodbye to Bogart without letting him know it would be forever. Jack leaned closer, and I forgot about his height. I realized what he had in mind. I was going to get kissed! I was too scared to breathe. I just waited as Jack moved closer and closer. Suddenly there was a face between ours, and Adam's deep voice whispered, "Knock it off."

Jack jumped about a foot out of his chair. I was so startled I turned around and yelled, "Hey!" Then everyone sitting around us started complaining. A couple of people yelled, "Shut up," and I was so embarrassed I wanted to sink down under my seat.

"My brother," I whispered apologetically, but Jack just stared straight ahead. His seat didn't creak again.

When we went next door for ice cream afterward, there was Adam with his date.

"Does he always follow you around like that?" Jack grumbled.

"Tell me more about Humphrey Bogart," I said, trying to cheer him up. He did and that took care of the conversation until it was time to go home.

Jack called his mother from the ice cream parlor to ask her to pick us up, and she arrived shortly. When we got to my house, I thanked her, and Jack walked with me up to the front porch. I tried to bend my knees and scrunch down a little so he wouldn't seem quite so short.

"I had a good time," I said. "It was really a good movie."

I knew he wasn't going to kiss me because his mother could see us from the car, but just then the porch light went on, and I'm sure it had a thousand-watt bulb in it. It was like a searchlight. The front door opened, and Rick stood there.

"Hi," he said. "I thought I heard you come home."

Jack staggered backward and almost fell off the porch.

"I'm Charlie's brother, Rick." He moved closer to Jack and stared down at the top of his head.

"How many brothers have you got?" Jack asked me as he took a step backward.

"Two," I said.

"Are you sure? It seems like a lot more."

"They just take up a lot more space than they should," I said. "Do you want to come in, Jack?"

"No, thanks," Jack said. "My mother's waiting." He kept moving backward until he was down the steps and hurrying toward the car. I just sighed and followed Rick into the house.

The next day on our way home from school I told Nancy what had happened.

"I'll never date again," I said. "I may as well give up thinking about Mark Potter."

"Of course you'll date," Nancy assured me, "and someday it will be Mark. We'll think of something."

We said goodbye at the corner near my house where Nancy turns off, and I crunched some dead leaves on the sidewalk, wishing I could give my brothers a good kick.

"What's the matter, Charlie?"

The voice startled me, and I jumped. Andy was sitting on our front steps. As I stared at him, he repeated the question.

He really looked interested, different from the times he and Rick used to tease me. So I sat on the porch steps next to him and told him my troubles—all of them, including how much I wanted Mark Potter to ask me for a date. Maybe Andy could get Rick and Adam to bug off. It was worth a try.

When I finished, Andy said, "As I see it, you need a guy to ask you out who isn't afraid to stand up to your brothers, and a way to date without their interference."

"I guess that's it."

Andy gave a long stretch and yawned. "No problem."

I turned and stared at him. "What do you mean, 'no problem'? It may not seem like much to you, but it's a big enough problem to ruin my life!"

"Calm down," he said. "No problem, because I've got the solution." He grinned as I continued to stare at him.

"One of the advantages of being a high-school senior is knowing a lot about what goes on."

I had my mouth open for a smart answer when he said, "So I happen to know something about this Mark what's-his-name that you don't know."

"What are you talking about?"

"About the casting for the school musical. They're auditioning for *Mame* right now. I'm going to be doing the lighting for the show, so I've been following the auditions. Mark Potter tried out for the chorus, and I heard that he got in. Tomorrow they're auditioning for the parts."

I sat up straight. "So! Mark is going to be in the school musical!"

Andy leaned forward. He took my shoulders and gave me a little shake. "Charlie, think! This is your big chance. Your dream is to be in musicals. Here's a good place to start."

I pulled back. "How do you know what my dream is?"

"It was some of the stuff you wrote in your diary."

"You and Rick! You horrible—"

"Keep quiet and listen," Andy insisted. "That was years ago, when we were a lot younger. It doesn't matter now. What matters is that you can really sing. The whole neighborhood has heard you singing around the house for years. You have a really terrific voice! You can audition for a part, and I think once Mr. Gallen hears you sing, you'll be in."

"But the seniors get all the good parts."

"OK, you might have to settle for a small part. Is that so bad?"

As the idea began to sink in, I could picture Mark and me together every evening. I'd think of clever things to say to him. He'd really notice me. We'd talk a lot. We'd practice the songs together. And then—maybe—he'd ask me out!

"Andy," I shouted, "you're wonderful!" I hugged him, wondering if I could talk his mother and mine into trading sons. Andy would be a terrific big brother.

"You know what they say in show business," Andy joked. "Break a leg."

When I went to the auditorium the next day to audition, I almost wished I had.

Chapter Seven

As I walked into that auditorium, I was scared. I don't know what I expected an audition to be like, but this wasn't it. The whole front of the auditorium was filled with people, all talking to each other. I saw somebody waving at me. It was Mark! I waved back, and I could feel my heart starting to beat faster. He was sitting over at the side with a bunch of kids who'd all made the chorus. I guess they just came to see who would audition for the main roles.

Why had I signed up to audition? I wished I'd gone with Nancy to watch the junior varsity practice. I wished I'd gone straight home after classes were out. I wished I was sitting at the kitchen table eating the cream out of the middle of a stack of Oreos and doing my algebra homework.

I started to get out of my seat but fell back into it as Andy stretched his long legs over me and climbed into the seat next to mine.

"I don't think I belong here with all these juniors and seniors," I told him.

"You're scared," he said.

"I'm terrified."

"Most actors are scared. I read about some who get so upset and nervous they throw up before every performance."

I just glared at him. "That's supposed to make me feel better?"

Andy shrugged. "What are you frightened about? You've got a good voice."

I stared down at my books. "The idea of getting on that stage and singing at all those faces scares me."

"Is that all?" he asked. "Don't worry about it."

"It doesn't help to just tell someone not to worry," I began, but Andy interrupted me.

"Don't look around to your right," Andy said. "That kid you like—the one named Mark—is watching you."

"He is?"

"If you run out now, you'll lose your big opportunity to see him every day while the show's in rehearsal."

"OK," I said slowly. "I'll stick it out."

"Good." He got up and climbed over me.

I grabbed for his hand and held it just for a second. "Keep your fingers crossed for me—OK?"

By this time Mr. Gallen was rapping on the top of the piano that stood below the stage. He was a short, round man with more hair in his mustache than on his head.

"Quiet down!" he shouted. "We've got to get busy. Mrs. Yolinski is here to provide piano accompaniment for the vocalists. If you've got sheet music, bring it to her."

Oh, no! Sheet music? I never used sheet music. I learn songs from recordings. I turned to tell Andy this, but he had gone.

Mr. Gallen read off a lot of names, and mine was third.

"Get up on the stage, Brooke," he said to a tall girl who was so pretty that if he'd added "Shields" I wouldn't have been surprised.

Mrs. Yolinski, whose tight permanent vibrated like little springs when she moved, began to play, and Brooke sang. It was a song from *Camelot*, and Brooke was all right, but nothing spectacular. However, when she finished, Mr. Gallen and Mrs. Yolinski nodded to each other and looked pleased.

Rita Cameron was the next girl up, and again Mrs. Yolinski led into the song. This time it was a Barbara Mandrell song, and Rita was all right, but Mandrell was a whole lot better.

Mr. Gallen called my name, and then he had to call it again, because my knees were so shaky I could hardly get out of my seat.

I managed to walk down the aisle to the

steps leading to the stage and start up them when Mrs. Yolinski asked, "Where's your music?"

"I'll have to sing without it," I told her.

She just shrugged as though they could write me off without wasting their time hearing me.

I walked to the center of the stage, took a deep breath, and stared down at all those faces. That's all I did. Just stared. I couldn't move.

Mr. Gallen said, "Well, Charlene? What are you going to sing?"

I must have been holding my breath. Nothing came out.

Andy yelled from a spot up near the ceiling of the auditorium, somewhere toward the back, "Hey, Mr. Gallen, you mind if I try out these lights while she's singing?"

And whap! I was in a spotlight so intense that I couldn't see beyond the edge of the stage. The brightness that surrounded me cut off all the faces. There was no one there but me. Maybe this was what Streisand felt like when she was on stage in the middle of all those spotlights, I thought. If Streisand could do it—well, how about me? I'd have to try.

I opened my mouth and let go. Nobody, but nobody, was going to rain on my parade!

As soon as I had finished, the light snapped off. Someone over on the right side of the auditorium applauded. I hoped it was Mark. A few others picked up the applause.

"You have quite a voice!" Mr. Gallen said. "Quite a good voice, young lady."

"Thank you," I said, smiling happily. Now that the worst was over, I felt great.

He gave Mrs. Yolinski a long look, then turned to his sheet. "Susan Gamill," he read.

I hurried off the stage as Susan climbed on. I was so glad to be back in my seat that I didn't even hear Susan sing. It startled me when Mr. Gallen called out the next name.

I decided that Andy must have found what he needed to know about the lights because he didn't turn them on again. Then it dawned on me what Andy had done. He had simply removed that sea of faces that had scared me so much. Now that was the kind of guy I'd like for a brother.

There were some good singers in the group, and some who were not very good. When he got to the end of the list, Mr. Gallen said everyone could leave. He'd have a callback on Friday, and those asked to audition again would find their names posted on the bulletin board outside the drama department.

As I hurried out of the auditorium, I looked around for Andy, but he was nowhere in sight. Maybe if I waited just a few minutes he'd come out, and I could thank him.

It was Mark who came out, not Andy. "I just wanted to tell you that you were great. Even without music. I guess it's because you sing so loud."

"Thanks," I said, and felt myself blush. Why did I get this weird feeling every time I was near Mark?

"I bet you'll get a part," he said.

"Thanks," I said. Then I went blank again. I looked at Mark, and I couldn't think of another word to say. Here we were, standing all alone, having a wonderful conversation, only there wasn't going to be any conversation if I couldn't think of something to talk about.

"I'd better get back inside," Mark said.

"I guess so."

"Well, I'll see you."

"Sure," I answered.

After he left I thought of some marvelous things to say. I thought of witty, bright remarks all the way home. But it was too late.

As I went into the kitchen Mom joined me. She had just come home after showing houses to clients all day. Her hug felt good, and I relaxed. She looked quickly through the mail she had brought in, then dropped it on the table.

"Anything from Dad?" I asked.

"Not today." She gave me a little smile, but I knew she was disappointed. Dad wrote to Mom almost every day, often enclosing letters to the rest of us. I hoped Dad's overseas job would be over soon. I missed him.

"How did the audition go?" Mom asked me.

"Mark was there. He told me I had a good voice."

Mom smiled. "What did Mr. Gallen say?"

"Oh, Mr. Gallen." I opened the cookie jar and took out a handful of Oreos. "He said I had a good voice. But he was nice to everyone. I think he was just trying to be polite."

"Want some milk with those cookies?" Mom asked.

"No, thanks." I flopped into the nearest chair. "Mom, I think I'd better learn to read sheet music."

"Then it might be a good time to start singing lessons. You've got a fine voice, and it could be even better with training." Mom paused only a second. "But you didn't tell me the most important thing. What about getting a part in the musical?"

"Mr. Gallen is having a callback on Friday. He'll put the names on the board. Mark's definitely going to be in the chorus."

"Well, let's hope you'll be in the play, too."

"Mom, Mark came out to talk to me after my audition, and I couldn't think of anything to say to him."

"Remember, I told you to be yourself. Then you'll be able to talk to the boys you're with."

I gave a long sigh. Who else could I be but myself? Mom's advice wasn't helping a bit.

Chapter Eight

On Friday morning I was walking to my first-period class when I saw Mark striding down the hall toward me. He smiled and stopped as I came up to him.

"Where have you been?" he asked.

"I don't know," I answered, desperately trying to think of something that made more sense.

"Haven't you seen the bulletin board?"

"Bulletin board?" This was Friday!

"Yeah," Mark said. "Your name is on the callback list."

"It is?" I knew my mouth was open, and I carefully shut it.

A bell clanged in our ears. "Good luck, Charlie," Mark said. "Let me know how you do."

People were pushing around us, and he moved off in the crowd. I'd been thinking so

67

much about Mark I'd forgotten about the names being posted. I elbowed my way down to the hall outside the drama department and stared at the sheet of typed names. There it was. My name. The callback was for that afternoon.

I don't know how I got through the day. Somehow the last bell finally rang, and I headed for the auditorium. Andy was waiting just inside the door.

"I knew you could do it," he said.

"Andy, I have to audition again."

He put a hand on my arm. "You're shaking."

"I'm still scared."

"I can't help you with lights this time," he said, "but I can teach you a trick. Think of the people in the audience in a silly situation."

"Like what?"

"Think of what they'd all look like if they were wearing Groucho Marx mustaches. Or sitting in mud puddles."

I giggled, and he added, "It works. I read about it."

"Wish me luck."

Andy shook his head. "I can't. That's bad luck." He grinned. "Break a leg, Charlie."

When we went into the auditorium, I was already more confident. There weren't as many people as before. Mr. Gallen had narrowed his list down quite a bit.

I looked around for Mrs. Yolinski, but she wasn't there. "I'd better tell you right away," I said to Mr. Gallen. "I don't read sheet music."

"We can work around that." He looked at his list again. "You're Charlene Carrington. Take a script from that pile over there and go over the part of Agnes Gooch. I want to hear you read in a few minutes."

"You don't want me to sing?"

"No. I know you can sing. Now I want to know if you can act."

As I read the script I began to remember the movie, which I'd seen when I was just a little kid. Agnes Gooch was a funny part. I was well into the script, enjoying it, when Mr. Gallen banged on the piano lid again.

This time he started with me!

"Charlene and Brooke. Get on stage, please."

We did, and he told us which scene he wanted us to read. I had never done anything like this before. I read the way I would read anything aloud, but Mr. Gallen interrupted us. "Charlene, do you hear what Brooke is doing? She's acting as she's reading. She's being Mame. Can you do that with your part?"

"I guess so," I said. I hadn't been paying much attention to Brooke because I was concentrating so hard on the lines I had to read.

As he walked back to his chair, Brooke whispered to me, "Did you see the movie?"

I nodded, and she said, "Then think about what Agnes Gooch was like. Try to be like Gooch when you're reading her lines."

Brooke started reading again, and I watched

her instead of staring at the script. She was being Mame, and she wasn't bad.

I kept staring at Brooke when she stopped, so I lost my place. "Yikes!" I said. However, I found it and tried what they had told me. I tried to be like Agnes Gooch, but I knew I wasn't very good. I must have improved a little bit, though, because Brooke smiled at me before she read her next line.

Finally Mr. Gallen stopped us. He didn't say anything, so I didn't know what he thought. He asked some other people to read different parts of the play. Then he had some other girls read Agnes Gooch's part. All this time I kept squirming in my seat and told myself I wasn't an actress anyway. The sooner this was over the better.

Mr. Gallen told us he'd post the cast list on the board early Monday morning. If I got a part, it was going to take every minute of my time. But I thought about being with Mark every evening. Mark was worth it.

I walked home alone thinking that here it was Friday, and again I wasn't going out. I wondered if using ESP on Mark would help.

Mom opened the door before I even got to the steps. She must have been watching for me. "Well?" she called out. "Did you get in the show?"

"He'll post the names Monday morning," I said.

She took a deep breath. "I guess we'll just have to wait."

I dropped my books on the sofa. "Mom, why do you care so much about it?"

Mom laughed. "Because I'm your mother and because being in a play is exciting and fun and a great way to meet some of the interesting people at school."

I just looked at her. Then I shook my head. "And it will keep me so busy I won't groan about not going out. Right?"

"Oh, Charlie," she said, giving me a hug, "you'll have lots and lots of dates while you're growing up."

"Promises, promises," I said as I headed toward the telephone to report to Nancy.

Later, Mom told Rick and Adam that I had been called back for a second audition. I was surprised at their reactions, which are usually negative.

"That's great!" Rick said. "Maybe you'll get a leading role."

"You do have a good singing voice, Charlie," Adam remarked.

It made me feel good that my brothers were happy for me. They usually teased me about my voice.

But then Adam said, "Charlie, be sure to give us a schedule of your rehearsal times, if you get in."

"Why?"

"Because if you're rehearsing at night, we'll have to pick you up."

"Mom?" It was more like a plea than a question.

"Adam is right," Mom said. "You certainly can't come home alone in the dark."

"Maybe I could get a ride with—with a friend," I said.

"That's a little chancy." Mom smiled at Adam. "I think it's thoughtful of your brothers to watch out for you."

When I told Nancy about it later, she said, "Oh, rats!"

That's the way I felt, too.

Chapter Nine

Saturday afternoon Nancy and I went to the mall, where a lot of the kids hang out. Nancy had to buy her father a birthday present, and she couldn't think of anything he needed.

As I sidestepped a baby stroller that was headed for my shins, I said, "Why don't you ask him what he wants?"

"I did, and he said he wanted earmuffs to wear in the house. Then he laughed like he had said something funny."

"Get him a tie," I said. I nearly bumped into her as she suddenly stopped to stare into a store window filled with briefcases.

"I always get him ties. Did you ever notice that fathers, in particular, have weird senses of humor?"

I sighed. "I know what you mean. I just

wish my father would get through with that job and come home. I'd even enjoy his dumb jokes. I miss him." For some reason I suddenly remembered a time, when I was just a little kid and there was a big mud puddle in the backyard. Rick had pushed me in the mud, and I was slinging big globs of mud at him for all I was worth.

"Oh, dear. She's turning into such a tomboy," Mom had said, but Dad had just laughed.

"Charlie's OK," Dad had said. "She's learning to stand up for herself."

"I wonder if any of those briefcases are under ten dollars," Nancy said, jarring me back to the present.

"You know they aren't."

"Wishful thinking, I guess. Let's find a store that sells ties."

"If my father were home, he'd do something about Rick and Adam," I said.

"You can't just wait for your father to come home. If you get picked for the musical, you'll have to think of something right away."

"If."

"You'll find out Monday," Nancy said.

"If I live that long."

Well, I did, and Monday morning I got to school early just to see that bulletin board. There were students crowded around it, and I had to squeeze in, ducking under a couple of elbows. I looked at the list of names for the chorus. Mark's name was there. I glanced quickly at the names for the main roles, but didn't see mine.

I started to turn away, so disappointed I couldn't think straight, when someone grabbed my shoulder and said, "Hey, congratulations, Charlie!"

It was Andy.

I guess I must have looked as puzzled as I felt because he said, "Didn't you see your name up there? You got the part of Agnes Gooch!"

"Andy!" I gasped. "I don't believe it!"

"Look for yourself."

I stared at the board, but all the letters wiggled around and made no sense at all. I tried to calm down and just read the list slowly. Sure enough, there was my name!

"I thought my acting was terrible," I said to Andy.

"Yeah, you weren't very good," Andy said, "but Mr. Gallen will work with you. It was your singing voice that got you the part."

Slowly everything began to sink in. "I'll be in rehearsals. Every night."

"You'd better be."

I started to grin. "With Mark!" I had to find Nancy.

Someone stopped to talk to Andy, and I rushed off. I met Nancy near her locker, where she was talking to Jed.

"Did you?" she asked.

"I did! I did!"

We began jumping up and down and hugging each other.

"What happened?" Jed asked, as we stopped for breath.

"I'm Agnes Gooch." I took a couple of deep breaths and pulled a strand of hair out of my mouth.

"Aw, come on," Jed teased. "I know who you are."

"You're Agnes Gooch?" Nancy shrieked. "Really?"

"Naw," Jed said to Nancy. "She's only kidding you. She's your friend Charlie."

"Very funny," Nancy said to Jed. "I'll see you at lunch period."

The first bell rang. "OK," Jed said good-naturedly, and he walked down the hall.

"I'll talk to you later," I told Nancy, and hurried down the hall toward my classroom.

Something happened in Mr. Hartman's life skills class that day that helped me sort things out.

"We're going to begin a section today on goal-setting and ways of reaching our goals," he told the class. He gave us an extra warm smile. Mr. Hartman was always into new stuff, and he made it so interesting that everybody liked being in his classes.

"What kind of goals are we talking about?" he asked us.

No one answered.

"Think. What are you working for? Reaching toward? Hoping for?"

"Christmas vacation," somebody mumbled.

Some guys in the corner started to snicker, and Mr. Hartman quickly said, "How many of you are planning to go to college?"

A lot of the hands went up. He wrote "college degree" on the board.

"And what will that degree do for you?"

When there was silence, he said, "It will be a step toward the job goals you have set for yourselves. Right? And you'll have other goals—perhaps marriage, children."

"That's a long time from now," Gordon Johnson piped up.

It seemed to be the right thing to say because Mr. Hartman smiled. "Very good, Gordon. We've talked about long-term goals. But there are short-term goals, too. Let's make a list of goals we may want to reach within the next few months or weeks, or even days."

I hoped he wouldn't go around the room and ask each of us, as he sometimes does when he wants a lot of answers. I couldn't think of any short-term goals. All I wanted was to date Mark Potter without my brothers around. I sat up straight as the thought hit me. Hey! Maybe I'd learn something useful that would help me!

No one had answered Mr. Hartman, so he said, "We'll go around the room, starting with the row by the window, and I want each of you to come up with at least one short-term goal."

Gordon was first. "I'd like to get a job after school in the hamburger place near the mall."

Gordon was certainly saying the right thing because Mr. Hartman beamed. "Is this a goal in itself, or is it a step toward a larger goal?"

"Huh?"

"I mean, do you want the job in order to earn money so that you can get something else—another goal?"

"I guess so," Gordon said. "My dad said he's not paying for my social life. If I'm going to date, I've got to earn the money myself."

Mr. Hartman nodded and turned to Becky next.

"I want to learn how to ski," she said. "Is that a goal?"

"Yes," he said.

"And I want to go to Aspen or Sun Valley, and I want to get a new ski outfit I saw in a magazine, and—"

Mr. Hartman shook his head. "Wait, Becky. Let's just stick with the ski lessons for now."

"But you told Gordon that—"

"We'll get back to your skiing goals later."

He came to me. "Charlene?"

I had no idea what to say. I suppose I thought that being honest might help, so I stammered, "My goal is to get my big brothers out of my hair."

A couple of kids laughed. Mr. Hartman just waited.

"I don't mean anything terrible," I explained.

"They think that because our dad is working overseas for a few months they have to take his place, and they're bugging me."

"Hmmm," Mr. Hartman mused. "Well, that's an unusual short-term goal. But it's feasible. Yes, I think we could say that gaining independence is a legitimate goal."

He called on Scott Firth, who sits in back of me, and I slumped in my seat. Why did I have to blurt that out? Why couldn't I have said something simple, like I wanted to earn the money to get a new sweater? Most people were coming up with goals concerned with things they wanted to buy. I tuned them out after a while. I wished the bell would ring.

But just before it did, Mr. Hartman said, "I want each of you to keep a personal, private notebook. Write your goal at the top of the first page. And jot down problems that might keep you from your goal. Tomorrow we'll discuss ways in which you might tackle your problems."

Now I was glad I'd been honest. Who knows? Perhaps his suggestions could help.

All day long people told me they heard I was going to be Agnes Gooch, and they either congratulated me or made some dumb joke about it. I began to get more and more excited. I was going to be in the school musical! Me!

As soon as school was out, I hurried home and told Mom. She was so excited she got on the phone and called Aunt Evelyn.

I tried to do my homework, but I couldn't

keep my mind on it. I kept thinking of seeing Mark and what I would say to him and what he would say to me. I made a little list of things to talk about on a scrap of paper that I could keep in my hand:

(1) Ever see *Mame*?
(2) Seen any movies lately?
(3) What kind do you like?

I hoped that the movie questions might make him think about taking me to see one. I also made a note to ask him about Seattle and how he felt about the move to Eagle River.

And I started my notebook for Mr. Hartman's class. Under problems that might get in the way of my goal-reaching, I wrote that my brothers were trying too hard to protect me. How I was going to find a solution for that one I didn't know. Maybe Mr. Hartman's life skills class would give me a clue.

Chapter Ten

Rick and Adam didn't show up until dinner time. Mom gave them the news.

Adam actually stopped eating and stared at me. "You got a real part!" he said. "That's great! They usually give those to seniors."

"Agnes Gooch? It's typecasting," Rick said. "What time are your rehearsals?"

"I don't know."

"You must know what time you're supposed to be there," Mom said.

"That part I know, but I don't know when they're over, so I'll just get a ride home with someone," I added quickly.

"That won't work," Adam said. "Suppose you couldn't get a ride and had to walk home in the dark? It's not safe."

"I remember last year when I was dating a

girl in the musical," Rick said. "Rehearsals got out around nine-thirty at first, and then Mr. Gallen began to go bonkers as they got closer and closer to opening night. Rehearsals got out later and later."

"We'll be there," Adam said. He reached for the meat loaf and began telling Mom about something that happened at football practice.

I just looked at my brothers and thought, OK! Wait until Mr. Hartman and I get through with you!

Before I left for rehearsal I wrote in my notebook: Complication is that my brothers are really pigheaded and think they know everything.

Adam drove me to the auditorium at seven. I didn't talk to him the whole way, but he didn't talk to me either, so my wounded silence didn't work very well.

A lot of kids were going in through the side door of the auditorium, and I went with them. I kept looking for Mark. There were an awful lot of people in this play.

Brooke came down the aisle. "Charlene, you'd better find a seat down in front. Mr. Gallen is going to give his pep talk in a few minutes."

Just as she finished, Mr. Gallen rapped on the piano. "Everyone in the back please move up closer."

I saw Mark then. He was with the guys moving up. Mr. Gallen waited until all the shuffling and mumbling stopped. Then he told us we were a team and we were going to put on the best musical in the history of the school. He talked about readings and blockings and a lot of stuff I had never heard of before.

There was more about getting measured for costumes and memorizing lines. Someone handed me a script and some sheet music and told me to work hard.

Then Mr. Gallen introduced Mrs. Yolinski as choreographer as well as accompanist. He said she would be working all next week with the chorus.

Mr. Gallen went over the rehearsal schedule again, and told the chorus and all the principals—I found out that's what those of us who had parts were called—to begin memorizing our music and scripts and be there promptly at seven the next night for our first reading..

But even before Mr. Gallen had finished, Rick and Adam showed up. They began talking to Andy over at the side of the stage. Mark left with some kids who were going out for sodas. I was left with my brothers. But before I followed them out, I took Andy's hand for just a second and squeezed it. "Thanks," I whispered. "If it weren't for you, I wouldn't be here tonight."

"Any time," he said, squeezing back.

Memorizing a script and learning how to act aren't easy. Brooke was about the only one in the play who knew what she was doing. I didn't get to talk to Mark because he was always with the chorus, and they were working in another section of the auditorium. And every night my brothers were there to pick me up.

At least Mr. Hartman's goals project was helping. "Be specific," he said as he leaned against the desk and glanced around the classroom. "Don't generalize. State your problems in specific terms."

"What does that mean?" Gordon asked.

I knew. I had lots of specifics. It was just a matter of picking and choosing. It wouldn't help to drag up all the problems of the past. The present was what was most important. I had written: "Every night my brothers come to pick me up at the auditorium after rehearsals. They'll scare off Mark if he wants to ask me out."

"If you have a good, specific problem then think of some way to solve it," Mr. Hartman had said.

How could I possibly solve that problem? My brothers were suspicious of everyone. They wouldn't approve of anyone else taking me home.

But a thought struck me that was so startling I nearly jumped out of my seat. There *was* someone Adam and Rick would approve of! Someone who said he'd do anything for me! Andy!

I'd ask Andy if I could ride home with him every evening. He lived right next door, so it made a lot of sense.

"On page three write down ways in which you might take care of your specific problems, keeping in mind that you are moving toward your goals," Mr. Hartman told us.

I wrote down that I was going to ask Andy.

Chapter Eleven

"Sure," Andy said when I caught up to him backstage that night. His eyes twinkled, and he looked as though he wanted to laugh.

"It's not funny," I told him. "Mark is never going to ask me for a date with Adam and Rick here night after night." I thought a moment. "You know something, Andy, Mark is awfully hard to talk to."

"Maybe you should ask him about his family or something like that," Andy suggested. He tucked a screwdriver into his pocket and rubbed his hands down the legs of his jeans.

"I don't mean that way. I mean that he's always with the chorus."

"How did I get so involved with your love life?" Andy asked. "Can't Mark do anything for himself? Asking you for a date shouldn't be that hard."

"Oh, Andy!" I leaned against the edge of the nearest backdrop and nearly fell over as it swung away from me. He grabbed my arms and kept me on my feet.

"What I was trying to say," I sputtered, "is that Mark hasn't asked me for a date because my brothers have scared off all the guys."

"Any guy who is worth anything could find a way to get around your brothers."

"But I have to let Mark know I'm interested in him first. So I need a chance to talk to him."

Andy just shrugged. "OK, Charlie. I'll see what I can do."

"Thanks," I said. "You've been so nice to me, and I appreciate—"

Andy looked at his watch. "Sorry, Charlie. I have to get busy on those lights. See you later."

I wished he hadn't rushed off like that. There was a lot more I wanted to tell him.

Mr. Gallen began rapping on the piano again. We joined him in front of the stage, where he stood with his arm around a boy who looked about nine or ten years old.

"This is my nephew, Billy," Mr. Gallen said. "We've persuaded him to take the part of young Patrick in the play."

It was easy to see that persuasion hadn't come easily because Billy scowled at everyone as he was introduced.

Brooke beamed at Billy. "Do you like to act?" she asked him.

"I hate it," he said. I had to laugh.

Mr. Gallen turned to me. "Charlene, since Billy's mother doesn't want him up too late, we'll go through your opening scene with him. Come in stage right, holding Billy's hand."

Billy and I went backstage. I reached for his hand, but he pulled it away and stuffed it in his pocket.

"Are you ready?" Mr. Gallen called.

"Take my hand, Billy."

He looked so wicked that I knew what was coming. I'd grown up seeing that look on my brothers' faces. Billy quickly pulled his hand from his pocket and put it into mine, along with something cold and rubbery. Did he think he was going to fool me with a toy snake?

I glanced down at our hands. "Too bad it's not a real snake. My last one died."

Billy looked so confused it was hard for me to keep a straight face. He didn't even try to pull his hand away. "You had a snake?" he managed to ask.

"Sure," I said. "Lots of them. But they all died."

"How did they die?"

I leaned down and looked at him nose to nose. "I ate them! And that's when I was in a good mood. Now put that snake back in your pocket and take my hand."

"Charlene and Billy?" Mr. Gallen called.

"Ready," I called back.

We went through the scene a few times, and Billy behaved himself—for then. However, I was having a problem with my acting.

"Charlene, you seem to have captured Gooch's awkwardness pretty well," Mr. Gallen said to me.

"Thanks," I answered, wondering what he was talking about.

"But the way you deliver your lines is somewhat wooden. We'll have to work on that."

Billy snickered.

"We'll go through your first song after we take a break," the teacher added. He beamed at Billy. "Billy has a fine singing voice."

"Yechh," Billy muttered.

I sat on the edge of the stage during the break. Mark came down the aisle from the back of the auditorium and stood in front of me.

"Hi," I said, thinking how handsome he was.

"Hi."

I wasn't prepared for this meeting, and I didn't have my notes. "Hi," I said again in sort of a whisper.

"Andy told me you wanted to talk to me," Mark said.

I could feel my face getting hot. "He shouldn't have done that," I stammered. "I just mentioned to him that I never got a chance to see you. That is, I just thought maybe we could get to know each other better. Uh—I mean—" I didn't know what I meant, so I stopped talking.

Mark looked toward the piano where Brooke was chatting with Rita. Brooke was brushing her long blond hair, and it glittered in the light. "After rehearsal Friday night, would you like to get something to eat?" Mark asked.

I was so surprised that at first I thought he was talking to Brooke, so I didn't answer. Finally he turned to me. "Well? Would you?"

"Uh—sure."

"OK."

I had rehearsed this moment in my mind for a long time. It wasn't coming out right. Mark didn't act very interested. But if he wasn't interested, why had he asked me out?

I groaned.

"Something the matter?" Mark asked me.

"Did Andy tell you to ask me?"

"Not exactly."

"What does that mean?"

"He just said you were kind of hoping I'd ask you out."

I groaned again, wishing I could sink through the floor. "You didn't have to. I'll probably kill Andy before Friday night, and then I'll be in jail, so I couldn't go out with you anyway."

Mark leaned against the stage and looked up at me. "I don't know what you're upset about. I kind of liked the idea that you wanted to go out with me."

"You did?"

"Yeah," he said. "I was going to ask you out a couple of weeks ago, but some of my friends told me about your brothers, so I didn't. Anyway, Andy told me not to worry."

"You really don't have to ask me out," I said again, but I could feel a smile growing. It was working out right! Everything was going to be wonderful!

"I already did," Mark pointed out, "and you told me you'd go. We have a date Friday night. OK?"

"OK."

"Well, break is almost over," Mark said.

"See you Friday," I managed to blurt out.

"I'll be here tomorrow, as usual."

"Oh," I said, watching him walk away.

The more I thought about Friday night the more excited I got. It really didn't matter how or why Mark asked me for a date. The fact was that he had! My dreams were coming true! What could go wrong?

I found out a few minutes later from Mr. Gallen.

Chapter Twelve

Mr. Gallen rapped on the piano again. I wondered what the life span for a piano with a banged-up lid was. He ought to blow a whistle like the coach does.

Mrs. Yolinski wiggled into place at the piano bench and looked up expectantly.

"Charlene," Mr. Gallen said while he was beaming at Billy, "let's just run through the 'Saint Bridget' song you sing with Billy."

"OK," I said, and swung my legs back up on the stage. Billy clumped up the steps to join me.

"You ever see a live rat up close?" he muttered as I took his hand again.

"The big kind, with sharp teeth?"

"Yeah." He tried to look as though he knew something I didn't know, but it didn't work well because he still hadn't figured me out.

However, I knew something he didn't know, and that was how to deal with little boys.

"Are you ready?" Mr. Gallen asked.

"Tell you what," I whispered to Billy. "Tomorrow you bring your rat, and I'll bring mine, and we'll see which one is the meanest."

"Ready?" Mr. Gallen repeated.

"Ready!" Billy said.

I knew what the phrase "striking a chord" meant after I saw Mrs. Yolinski in action. She didn't show that piano any mercy. She played the overture, and on cue I went into action.

I was really getting into the music when Mr. Gallen raised his hands. "Stop, Charlene!" he said.

"What's the matter?" I asked.

He looked a little puzzled. Mrs. Yolinski stared at me and then at her piano and frowned. One of us wasn't working right.

"It's your delivery of the song, Charlene," he said. "You're taking care of little Patrick. You're in a strange city, looking for Mame's address on Beekman Place. You're lost and lonely and afraid. Keep this in mind, and let's try it again."

Mrs. Yolinski attacked the piano, and I started the song over again. I hadn't got very far into the lyrics when Mr. Gallen shook his head and waved his arms again. "No, no, no." He rubbed his chin for a moment. "Your delivery. It reminds me of someone."

"Barbra Streisand," Billy piped up. "Only louder."

"That's it!" Mr. Gallen said. "Are you aware, Charlene, that you're singing this song the way Barbra Streisand sings and that it just doesn't fit?"

"I'm not trying to sing like Barbra Streisand."

"But you're doing it," Billy said.

"Perhaps unconsciously," Mrs. Yolinski added.

"Mama," Billy called to a woman sitting over at the side of the auditorium, "I wanna go home."

"I'll try again," I told Mr. Gallen.

"I have to go to the bathroom," Billy called out.

"Billy, aren't you going to be cooperative?" Mr. Gallen asked him.

"No," Billy said. "It's past my bedtime."

"The poor lamb is probably tired," Mrs. Yolinski said.

Billy's mother climbed out of her seat. "I'll bring him back tomorrow," she told Mr. Gallen. "When he's tired, it's hard to do anything with him."

"Very well," Mr. Gallen said. "We'll move along to Vera and Mame's song, 'Bosom Buddies.' "

I jumped off the stage and walked to the seats in the shadows near the back of the auditorium. There I slumped down where no one could see me. I knew I needed a lot of direction with my acting, but I couldn't understand what was wrong with my voice. I thought if I could do anything, it was sing. But it wasn't right, and I didn't know what to do about it.

Someone plopped down next to me. "Is this seat taken?" Andy asked.

"I blew it," I told him. "Mr. Gallen doesn't like the way I sing."

"He likes the way you sing," Andy said. "That's why you got the part."

"But I'm not doing it right."

"That's because you're singing like Barbra Streisand."

"I'm singing like myself."

Andy leaned close to me, and I could smell the warm, spicy fragrance of his shaving lotion. "Who's the 'myself' you're talking about?"

"Me."

"When you're singing, who do you feel like?"

"Me, of course."

"Yeah? Think about it."

I let out a long sigh. "I sometimes think of what it would be like to be Barbra Streisand, I guess."

"Why don't you think about what it would be like to be yourself up there in the spotlight and then sing the way you would sing?"

"Andy," I wailed, "I don't know how!"

Andy thought a moment. Then he said, "As soon as we get home tonight, I think I can get you on the right track. And tomorrow Mr. Gallen won't have anything to complain about."

"You really can help me that much?"

"I think so."

"How?"

"Wait and see." He unfolded his long legs and stood up. "I have to get back up there and adjust a few more lights."

"Mark!" I said, nearly bouncing out of my seat. "That reminds me. You told him I wanted to talk to him, and you said—"

"Why didn't you talk to him?" Andy said. "I told you to ask about his family."

"Well, I—"

"You should have done what I told you."

"What's so important about Mark's family?"

"Never mind for now," Andy said. "It will give you something to talk about when you go out with him on Friday."

"OK." It wasn't until after he disappeared into the back of the auditorium that I realized I hadn't told Andy what I thought of him. He had done the same thing my brothers always did— got me so confused I was sidetracked. I was a little disappointed in Andy.

I scrunched down in my seat. As I listened to the others, I began to feel better. Mr. Gallen criticized everyone, so I knew I wasn't the only one who made mistakes.

I was surprised when Mr. Gallen looked at his watch and announced that rehearsal was over. Rick and Adam were standing near the side door, and I hadn't even seen them come in.

Everyone was clearing out and yelling good night as I joined my brothers.

"See you tomorrow, Charlie," Brooke said. Her smile was right out of a toothpaste commercial, and it went over my head, directly to Adam.

"Adam," I said. "Adam!" I yanked on his arm to get his attention.

The door had shut behind Brooke, so Adam slowly turned back and looked at me. "Ready to go?" he asked.

"For the last time," I said.

"You got kicked out of the play?" Rick asked.

"Don't be ridiculous," I said. "I mean after tonight I have a ride home." Before either of them could object, I said, "With Andy. He lives right next door. It makes sense."

Andy stepped up, stuffing his shirt into his jeans.

"Andy doesn't want to have to take you home every night," Rick said.

"I'll make the sacrifice," Andy offered.

"You don't have to be bothered," Adam told him. "Charlie isn't your kid sister."

"You can be thankful for that," Rick said.

"I am," Andy agreed.

"Then it's settled," I told them as I started

out the door. Rick and Andy began talking about some dumb thing that happened during football practice, and I gave a long sigh of relief.

Mission accomplished, Mr. Hartman, I thought. I was one step closer to my goal.

Chapter Thirteen

Andy drove into his driveway at the same time Adam steered his car into ours, and he was on our front porch before we had opened the door.

"Time for your singing lesson, Charlie," Andy said.

"What are you talking about?" Rick asked him.

"Charlie needs a voice coach. I volunteered for the job."

"You?" Rick and Adam both laughed. "You sing like a bullfrog with a head cold, and you're going to give Charlie voice lessons?"

Andy just stared at Rick eyeball to eyeball. "Go on inside, both of you," he said. "We've got to start the first lesson."

Adam's eyebrows shot up. "On the front porch? Now? She'll wake up the neighborhood."

"You guys don't know anything," Andy told them. "There are certain things she has to learn before she starts to sing. She won't get to the singing part until tomorrow."

"You're crazy," Rick said. "It's getting cold out here!"

Andy looked at his watch. "Come on, guys, my time is valuable, and you're wasting it."

Rick and Adam went into the house.

"Sit down, Charlie," Andy directed. "Are you warm enough?"

I nodded. It was a surprisingly mild day, and I had on a down-filled jacket. I sat on the top step. "Exactly what kind of a voice lesson is this going to be? How can I have a voice lesson if I can't sing?"

Andy sat down beside me, close to me, and I could feel the warmth of his body. I turned to look up at him. Tall, big-boned, rugged Andy. His deep brown eyes were looking into mine. I felt myself blushing and quickly glanced away. To steady myself I took a deep breath.

"We're just going to talk in this lesson," Andy said. "We're going to talk about how you can sing like yourself and not like somebody else."

I shrugged. "OK. You said you could help me. Except I really don't know how because I don't know of any other way to sing except the way I'm doing it."

"Close your eyes."

When I did, he said, "Now, picture yourself

on a stage in front of a lot of people. You're holding a mike and ready to sing. The band has started playing. You open your mouth and start to sing. You look and sound just like Linda Ronstadt."

"What?" My eyes flew open, and I turned and stared at him.

"Seems crazy, doesn't it?" Andy said.

"Of course it does."

"OK. Close your eyes again."

As soon as I did, he said, "All right. Get that same picture. You're ready to sing. You open your mouth and start to sing, and you're Barbra Streisand."

And I was.

"See what I mean?" Andy asked.

"How did you know how to do that, Andy?"

"Mr. Hartman's giving his senior class some work on what he calls 'imaging'—mental exercises to get what you want—stuff like that."

Good old Mr. Hartman!

"So now what do I do?"

"Close your eyes again." Andy shifted to get more comfortable and moved even closer. "Get the mental picture of yourself with the mike. See what you're wearing—something that you like and feel comfortable in. OK?"

"Got it," I said. "But couldn't I be wearing one of those gorgeous designer gowns that Bar—"

"You're doing it again," Andy interrupted.

I smiled. "OK. This time it's just me." I

pictured myself in my new blue dress. Andy had liked that dress.

"Now," Andy said. "We've got to get to the next step."

"What's that?"

"Keep quiet and listen."

"I feel funny sitting here in the dark with my eyes closed." It was a little bit like being scared, only I didn't know what I was scared of. I scooted even closer to Andy, but that didn't help a bit. Instead of feeling reassured by touching him. I felt that little electric shocks were running through me.

"Don't get nervous about it, or it will spoil everything," Andy said. "Here. Take my hand."

His hand was big, and he held mine firmly. *I kept my eyes closed and tried to stop trembling. Come on,* I told myself. *It's just Andy—good old big brother Andy.* I took a couple of deep breaths and made myself relax.

"When you're ready," Andy said, "picture yourself singing a song that Barbra Streisand never heard of. Just to play it safe, better think of a Kenny Rogers song. You'll never picture yourself as Kenny Rogers."

So I thought of a song and concentrated on the picture. "I've got on a cowboy hat now," I said.

"You're a tough one to work with," Andy said. "You're sure fighting not to be yourself."

"Why?" I asked.

"You tell me. Look down at your audience. Who do you see there?"

"Rick and Adam," I said without having to think. I looked through the audience. "And Nancy is there, of course, and Mom and Dad and—"

"Get back to Rick and Adam. What are they doing?"

"Staring at me."

"Tell them to leave."

I tried so hard I made a squished-up face. "They won't."

"You're in charge, Charlie. It's your mind. Just move them out the side door whether they want to go or not."

I tried it, and it worked. "I did it!"

"So now take a good look at yourself. It's you with that mike in your hand, Charlie, and nobody else. Right?"

"The cowboy hat is gone."

"Keep the picture, and just in your mind, sing to the audience."

It was hard to do. A couple of times Barbra Streisand suddenly came back. But I worked at the mental picture and finished the song. Finally, giving a big sigh, I leaned over against Andy's shoulder. "That was tough!"

"But you did it," he said.

"Will it work?"

"If you keep doing it. Practice getting that mental picture until there's no doubt in your mind who's doing your singing."

Andy looked at his watch again. "End of first singing lesson."

"Do you really think I can sing the way Mr. Gallen wants me to sing?"

"Sure you can," Andy said. "We'll work on it together." He pulled me to my feet.

"Andy," I said, "you'd make a terrific brother."

He didn't answer, just gave a kind of a chuckle.

"See you tomorrow," I said, and went inside.

That night, after I had climbed into bed, I practiced the mental exercise Andy had taught me. There I was, mike in hand, blue dress and spotlight. "Out," I said to my brothers, "and take this stupid cowboy hat with you!" They got up from their seats in the front row and left.

I can do it, I thought, and as I began to sing, I fell asleep.

The next morning at the breakfast table I told everyone about my date on Friday night. "He's a nice guy, and he's someone I've been wanting to go out with, and I'm not going to let anybody ruin it." I leaned across the table and glared at Rick and Adam so there wouldn't be any question about who I meant.

"What's his name?" Adam asked.

"Mark Potter," I said.

"Mark Potter?" said Rick. "Isn't he that new guy who just moved here from Seattle?"

"That's right," I said.

"Does he have two sisters named Allison and Joyce?" asked Adam. "They just moved here, too, and I think their last name is Potter. Allison's a junior, and Joyce is a senior. They're both great-looking girls."

"You can say that again," Rick agreed.

"But that doesn't mean that this Mark Potter can be trusted, even if he is their brother," said Adam. "We'd better meet him."

I stood up, throwing my napkin on my chair. "That does it!" I shouted. "The two of you have no right to butt into everything I do! You're like prison guards! You're like—like—Russian spies! You're—" Tears came to my eyes, and I brushed them away. It was always like this. I'd get so mad I'd start to cry and lose the argument, and then I'd get mad at myself.

"Where are you and Mark going?" Adam asked, as though I'd been talking to myself.

"What time do you plan to be home?" Rick grinned at me.

"Mom!" I said.

"That's enough," Mom said.

I kissed her goodbye and started off for school. I was determined that Mark and I were going to have a good time on this date, with no brothers around to bother us.

Chapter Fourteen

I spent a lot of time in school thinking about what Andy had taught me. Every once in a while, I would close my eyes for a few moments and picture myself singing as myself. I was even beginning to hear the sound of my voice, and I liked it. It was a lot more plain and simple than the Barbra Streisand voice I'd been using, but it was OK.

"Charlene," Mrs. Jensen said in English class, "are you taking a nap?"

"No," I said, giving her a big smile, "I was doing my homework."

She gave me a strange look, so I quickly bent over my paper and began to work on the theme we were supposed to be writing.

After school I hurried home, went into my bedroom and shut the door, then stood in front of the mirror over my dressing table. I closed my eyes, thought of myself in front of a mike, and began to sing. This time I sang out loud. I had to keep the picture strong, but I managed it.

I was almost through with my song when there was a rap on my bedroom door, and Mom poked her head through. She looked puzzled. "Charlie?" she asked.

"Yes, Mom?"

"You sounded different," she said. "I liked it. I've always loved hearing you sing, but this was special. This was—"

She stopped, and I finished her sentence. "This was me!"

"I guess that's it," she said. "It sounded more like you than the voice on the records you sing with."

So I told her about Andy and his first voice lesson. She laughed and said, "He's marvelous. Good for Andy."

"Yeah," I said. "Good old Andy." I felt warm and happy just thinking about him and what he had done to help me.

"Wait until he hears you sing tonight," Mom said.

"Andy's going to be happy," I said.

"I mean Mr. Gallen," Mom said.

"Him, too!" We both giggled. It wasn't until I was at rehearsal that it dawned on me that I hadn't been thinking of Mark at all.

Brooke came up to me as soon as I entered

the auditorium. "Your brothers are so thoughtful to take you back and forth to rehearsal every evening."

"Thoughtful? Yech! They're just trying to run my life."

She looked surprised. "Maybe you don't appreciate them because they're your brothers. They seem awfully nice to me."

"Oh, they're nice enough I suppose." I shrugged. "But they won't be picking me up anymore. Andy lives next door, so I'll be riding home with him."

Brooke looked disappointed.

Just then, Billy came up to me. He gave me a wicked look.

"Billy, my little friend," I said, gripping his shoulder and propelling him ahead of me, "let's go over here out of the way and have a nice chat."

As soon as we were off by ourselves, I said, "Turn out your pockets, Billy."

He did immediately, his eyes wide with innocence. "See? Nothing in them."

"You've got something in mind."

"You sound like my mother."

I tried a new approach. "Let's be friends Billy. OK?" I held out my hand.

He shook it, but there was still something in his eyes that made me wary.

"Let's try 'Saint Bridget' again," Mr. Gallen called to us. "Charlene, Billy, up on the stage."

Now was the time!

We got into position, and I closed my eyes for just a few seconds, bringing up the mental picture of myself before the mike. Unfortunately, I kept my eyes closed a second too long. As we stepped forward, Billy stuck out a foot, and I stumbled over it.

I managed to stay on my feet, and Mr. Gallen said, "Charlene, Gooch is awkward but not quite that clumsy. I think a simple entrance will be sufficient."

Billy snickered, and I gripped his hand tightly. I'd have to watch out for this kid every minute, I thought.

Mrs. Yolinski raised her hands high and slapped them down on the piano keys, banging out the opening notes to our song. I lifted my head, stood up straight, and sang. I was Charlie, nobody else, and I could sing!

At the right place Billy joined in. Mr. Gallen didn't stop us, so we sang the whole song.

"Fine," Mr. Gallen said. "We'll have to work on the plaintive quality we want, Charlie, but this was a good beginning. Billy, you were splendid."

Even Mrs. Yolinski smiled at me, and at the break Andy came by. "You did great, kid."

Mark waved before he left. "See you, Charlie." I felt wonderful.

When I got home I wrote on a note pad things I could talk about with Mark:

(1) rehearsals
(2) chorus?
(3) family?
(4) Seattle?

I wasn't sure why Andy wanted me to ask Mark about his family, but there must be a good reason.

Andy. I thought about Andy sitting on the porch with me, and those tingling feelings came back and scared me. "I've got a date with *Mark,*" I said aloud. I closed my eyes so I could see his handsome face. For sure Mark had to be the handsomest guy in our high school.

Friday night came in a hurry, I guess because I was so busy with school and homework and rehearsals. I wore my new skirt and blue sweater that night to rehearsal.

Nancy had picked out my outfit. "All men like the color blue, so wear your blue sweater. It looks great, now that your mom was able to get the ketchup out of it." She added, "Try not to order hamburgers. You know how they sometimes fall apart and drip into your lap."

I thanked Nancy for her sisterly advice by poking her.

Mark waited for me at the door after rehearsal. "I hope you don't mind walking," he said. "I haven't got my driver's license yet."

"That's OK, I walk all the time. I mean, everywhere I go I walk. That is—" I decided to change the subject in a hurry. I sounded like an idiot. "What do you think of the way the rehearsals are going?"

"Pretty bad. But Allison, my sister, says that's always the way it is. Everything shapes up toward the end."

We started down the street toward the shopping center.

"Why do you say the rehearsals are bad?" I asked Mark. "I thought we were all doing a pretty good job."

"Well, you sing fine, Charlie. I bet people could hear you a block away. I didn't mean you weren't OK. I just mean that things don't seem to be put together yet."

"We're just getting into it." I knew I sounded defensive, so I tried to think of something else to say. At that moment, though, I tripped over a broken chunk in the sidewalk, and Mark grabbed my arm.

"Thanks," I mumbled, wishing I were as graceful as Brooke.

"Watch where you're going," he said.

We came to the parkway and turned into the mall. "You like pizza, don't you?"

"I love pizza," I answered, clenching my teeth. I was so worried about handling those strings of cheese that I forgot what else I was going to talk about.

When we were seated in the pizza place, Mark ordered two Cokes and a pepperoni pizza with extra cheese. I felt so uptight I just stared at the tablecloth. We sat there without speaking for a few minutes. This wasn't the way my date with Mark was supposed to turn out. What would I tell Nancy?

That last thought cleared my head, I guess, because I remembered the list.

"Mark," I said so suddenly that he jumped, "tell me what it's like being in the chorus."

"I dunno."

"Oh," I said. Finally I added, "You all look like you're working real hard."

"Yeah, I guess so."

I was beginning to worry about the lack of excitement between us.

Our pizza came along with a couple of large Cokes. I tried to stall eating by taking big gulps of my drink, but I had to eat sometime.

Mark handed me a slice. I took a large bite—much too large. I tried to catch the sauce that was dribbling down my chin. Suddenly all those little bouncy strands of cheese came to life and wrapped themselves around my fingers.

"Pizza is very hard to eat politely," I said through all that mess, and we both laughed.

"Tell me about your family," I said to Mark, remembering the next item on my list.

"My mom is an accountant," he said.

"Mine's in real estate."

"And my dad works in a bank," he added. "And I've got two older sisters who are a real pain in the neck."

"I've got two older brothers—twins."

"I know," Mark said through a mouthful

of pizza. "But brothers wouldn't be as much of a problem as sisters."

"My brothers are always telling me what to do."

"So are my sisters."

"My brothers don't take me seriously."

"My sisters treat me like a little kid. And what's more they monopolize the bathrooms every morning. Once my dad had to go out to the garage to shave."

"How old are your sisters?"

"Sixteen and seventeen," he answered. "Allison's a junior, and Joyce is a senior."

"How do they like it here? In Eagle River, I mean."

"OK so far," he said.

All of a sudden, I remembered the conversation I'd had with Rick and Adam about Mark. They had seemed quite interested in his sisters. Suddenly, it occurred to me why Andy had suggested that I talk to Mark about his family.

"Tell me more about your sisters," I said. "I bet they're beautiful."

"They think they are."

I felt sorry for Mark. I guessed his sisters were as big a problem for him as Rick and Adam were for me. "It's tough being the youngest, isn't it?"

"Why don't we talk about something else?" Mark said.

"OK," I said, but I couldn't think of anything else to say.

We finished our pizza and started walking home. It's a long walk home from school, and even longer from the mall. I usually walk to and from school in the daytime, but my brothers strongly object to my walking at night. I figured I'd be safe with Mark, though.

Suddenly, I felt him stiffen. "What's the matter?" I asked.

"Someone's following us."

The street we were on was dark, and only a few houses had lights in the windows. I gasped. "Maybe we should run up on someone's porch and bang on the door and yell for help."

"Walk faster," Mark said. "He's coming closer."

I had to turn and look, even though Mark was pulling on my arm. A large, dark shape was moving up behind us.

But the shape looked familiar. "Adam!" I shouted. "Is that you?"

"Don't mind me," Adam called out. "I'm just walking home." We let him pass us, but the evening had suddenly gotten a lot less romantic.

Mark let go of my hand. "Your bodyguard."

"Honestly, Mark, it's just a coincidence," I told him. "If you ignore them, they go away."

"Everybody told me it would be like this," he said. "I know they're your brothers, but how do you stand it? Suppose I want to kiss you good night. Will they turn on a spotlight?"

I stared at him. Even in the dim glow of the streetlight, he was handsome. "Mark," I said, really touched, "do you want to kiss me good night?"

"I guess."

"Listen, Mark, I'd like to see you again. I have the beginnings of a plan in my mind—a plan that will take care of any problems with my brothers."

"C'mon, Charlie. Nothing's going to stop your brothers from watching over you."

"Will you take a chance?" I asked him.

He thought a moment. "OK."

We walked the rest of the way home without another word. But before he left, Mark kissed me gently on the lips. Miracle of miracles, the porch light didn't come on, and there wasn't a brother in sight. Unfortunately, there weren't any fireworks, either. After weeks of dreaming about this moment, I realized that Mark tasted more like pizza than romance.

Chapter Fifteen

The next morning was one of those great fall days in which the air seems to crackle and the leaves crunch when you step on them and the sun makes everything glow with a kind of a golden haze. I was in the backyard raking leaves, when Andy strolled over.

"Hi," I said. "Rick's at football practice."

"I know," he said. "Want some help?"

"I'm almost finished. Thanks, anyway."

"How about another singing lesson?"

I laughed.

"I'm serious," he said.

I stopped raking. "Andy, you've been hearing me sing at rehearsals. Has it been so bad?"

"It's been great, Charlie. I just thought we'd have another lesson. How's the mental exercise coming along?"

"It's working," I said. Then I thought of something I had to ask Andy. "Are Mark's sisters beautiful? I don't remember seeing them at school."

"What has that got to do with anything?"

"Are they?"

"Yes."

"I think Rick and Adam are interested in them."

"What's on your mind?" Andy asked.

"Last night Adam followed Mark and me and nearly scared us to death. I got an idea. If I could have a party and Mark and his sisters could come, Rick and Adam would be occupied with them. Then Mark and I could cut out and have a real date without my brothers being in the way. What do you think?"

"On a scale of one to ten, it's about a zero," Andy said.

I sighed and leaned back on the handle of the rake. "Why?"

"In the first place, you can't cut out on a party you're giving."

"I guess not. I hadn't thought of that."

"And in the second place, ever since they arrived in Eagle River, Mark's sisters have been dating a lot. They wouldn't go to a party given by a friend of their little brother."

"So the whole thing's no good."

"Not completely. Getting Rick and Adam together with Allison and Joyce is a possibility."

I sat up straight and stared at Andy. "What do you mean?"

"Maybe I could invite them over to my house for a party next Saturday."

"Do you think they'd come?"

"I can find out. But I wouldn't invite their little brother. You'd have to do that."

"I suppose I could. Last night I actually asked Mark not to give up on seeing me."

"He shouldn't have had to be asked."

"Andy," I said, "you're going awfully far, giving a party just to help me out."

"It's not just to help you. I've got other reasons."

"Like what?"

Andy reached over and tapped the end of my nose. "It's really none of your business, but I happen to like parties." He grinned. "And some people think Allison and Joyce Potter would come in ahead of Bo Derek."

Suddenly I didn't want to hear another word about Mark's sisters. I hadn't met them, but already I didn't like them. "I'm supposed to go over to Nancy's house this afternoon. I'd better finish up."

"Tell Nancy that if the party works out, she and Jed can come, too."

Andy walked back toward his house.

"Thanks, Andy. I'll keep my fingers crossed for it to work out." I wondered why the idea didn't sound as great as it had at first.

Nancy was excited when I told her later. "I

always thought Andy was a real pest, but lately he seems to have changed a lot for the better."

"I wish Rick and Adam would change for the better, too." I sat on the foot of her bed, hugging my knees to my chin.

"And he's really good-looking now. Have you noticed?"

"Who? Rick or Adam?"

"Andy."

I shrugged. "I guess I haven't noticed."

"I wonder who else will be at his party."

"I hadn't thought about anyone else being there."

"There have to be enough people, and everybody coming would bring a date."

"Oh. I guess so." For some reason all I could think of was who would be with Andy.

"You haven't told me the most important thing of all," Nancy said.

I must have looked as blank as I felt. "What important thing?"

"Your date with Mark," she said. "What happened?"

"We ate pizza."

For a moment she was silent. "Well, tell me about the good part."

Now it was my turn to be silent.

Finally Nancy said, "Well?"

"I'm trying to think of a good part. You know, nothing about that date was really great. We ate the pizza and walked home, and Adam was practically walking with us for a while. But after Adam was out of the way and Mark and I got to my house, he kissed me."

"He kissed you!" Nancy exclaimed. "And you say it like it was nothing! Weren't you excited?"

"It wasn't as exciting as I thought it would be. Maybe because I was wondering if Rick or Adam would suddenly show up."

"That's probably it," Nancy said. She patted my shoulder. "Just wait until Andy's party. Your problem will be solved."

"That's just an 'if.' "

Nancy pulled her sweater from under her bed and shook it out. "The trouble with you, Charlie, is that you don't think positive enough," she said. "Let's go to the mall and get a milk shake."

So we did. By the time Nancy had given me her pep talk I could hardly wait to see Mark again.

Chapter Sixteen

Nancy came over to our house and stayed for dinner. I cooked it because Mom had been out all day showing houses. While she rested I made a big tossed salad and chili dogs. Rick and Adam grumbled about that, but I didn't care. Last Christmas Rick had given me a cookbook, which I thought was a bad hint; so I gave it back to him on his birthday. Anyhow, Nancy was our guest, and she especially likes chili dogs.

"Are you going out tonight, Charlie?" Adam asked me as I passed him the jar of mustard.

"No." I was tempted to say more but thought I'd better stay cool in case I said too much. I didn't want them to know what Andy and I were planning. I wished Andy would call. It was driving me crazy wondering if he'd have the party.

That "no" just hung in the air until Nancy spoke up. "There's a real good movie on TV tonight. Charlie and I are going to watch it."

"Sounds real exciting," Rick said sarcastically.

"Mind your own business," I said.

Mom sighed. "Rick, are you going out tonight?"

"Yeah," Rick said.

"Where?"

"I've got a date."

"With whom?"

"You don't know her."

"Where are you going?"

"We haven't decided yet."

I bounced in my chair. "You see what I mean? That's the way Adam and Rick always act, and yet they think they have to know everything about me!"

"Charlie has a good point," Mom said. "I'd like to know where you boys are going tonight."

Adam put down his fork. "I'm going to meet some friends and go to a party." He scowled as he added, "I don't care if Brenda's at the party or not."

"Who's Brenda?" Mom asked.

"The girl I am—was—going with."

"I didn't know you were going with anyone special," Mom said.

"She wasn't that special." Rick laughed and ducked as Adam gave him a shove.

"How about that demented cheerleader you

went out with last week? On a scale of one to ten, she'd rate minus five," Adam teased.

"Yeah, well I'm not going out with her anymore," Rick shot back.

"Are you and Andy double-dating as usual?" Mom asked Rick.

"No. Andy's got a date with Allison Potter. He didn't want to double."

Adam looked interested. "Yeah? How did he manage that?"

Rick shrugged. "Just lucky, I guess."

So that was why Andy hadn't called me. He was probably going to ask Allison about the party. I know I should have felt good because Andy was working out the plan but instead I felt so awful I put down my second chili dog only half eaten and stared at my plate.

"What's the matter, Charlie?" Mom asked.

"I don't know," I said. I really didn't. I couldn't understand why I felt like this just because I found out that Andy was seeing the beautiful Allison.

"Rats," I muttered.

"So that's what we're eating. I knew it tasted funny," Rick said.

I convinced Nancy to go home early. Then I turned on the TV and flopped on the sofa in front of it.

Mom came in, wearing her robe and slippers and smelling damp and woodsy like her favorite perfumed soap. "What are you watching?"

I had no idea. "Mom, I really like Mark a lot."

"That's nice."

"I really do."

She turned to look at me. "Are you trying to convince me or yourself?"

"I'm not trying to convince anybody."

Mom settled back in a chair.

"I just thought I'd talk about it, Mom."

"Fine. What do you want to tell me?"

"Nothing."

"I thought you just said—"

"I did. But I just realized there isn't anything more to say about Mark. Not until we get to know each other better."

"How was your date with him after rehearsal yesterday evening?"

"Sort of OK."

Mom turned off the TV. "How can something be 'sort of OK'?" she asked, sitting down again.

"I mean we went to eat pizza, and he brought me home, and that's all there was to it."

"That sounds nice to me."

"It was, I guess, except for the cheese on the pizza, and I was wondering, Mom—"

"About what?"

I decided I'd better not mention the possibility of Andy's party or why he'd be giving it. It was all too complicated. Besides, I didn't want

128

to think of Andy out with Allison. I got up and turned the TV back on.

"If you want me to, I'll make popcorn, Mom."

She closed her eyes for a moment. "Charlie, I must be more tired than I thought I was. I seem to be having trouble following your train of thought."

I patted her hand. "You work awfully hard, Mom. I'll go make the popcorn."

The popcorn was full of hard kernels, the movie was terrible, and Andy didn't get in touch with me until two o'clock the next afternoon.

When I answered the phone, he said, "Party's all set for next Saturday night."

"Thanks, Andy."

"What's the matter? You don't sound as glad as I thought you would."

"Sure I'm glad." I couldn't keep from adding, "Rick said you went out with Allison Potter last night."

"That's right."

The silence began to get uncomfortable, so I stammered, "Is it—could I—that is, would it be all right if I invite Nancy to the party now?"

"Sure," he said. "And Mark."

"Oh, that's right. I'll have to ask Mark."

"I thought that's what the party was all about."

"It is. I mean I have to get my courage up to ask him, and there's always the chance he can't go."

"Think positive," Andy said. "After I say

goodbye, hang up the phone and close your eyes and picture yourself at the party with Mark."

"The mental exercises?"

"Right. Goodbye." There was a click as he hung up.

Slowly I put down the phone and did as Andy said. With my eyes closed I pictured Mark standing next to me in Andy's den. There were some faceless couples dancing in the background to one of Andy's records, and the lights were not too bright. I was wearing my white dress with the wide red belt, and I looked pretty good.

Mark was standing beside me, eating a chunk of chocolate cake and watching the dancers.

"Pay attention to me," I told him.

"I'll get you some cake," he said, and he turned to walk away.

I used all my powers of imaging and brought him back to my side without the cake.

I opened my eyes and gave a big sigh. This imagining didn't always work out the way it was supposed to. Maybe I needed more practice. Maybe I'd better just call Mark and get step one over with.

His family wasn't listed in the phone book yet so I got it from information, then dialed it. I felt very nervous as I waited for someone to answer.

Finally a soft, breathy voice said, "Hello?" It was the kind of voice Nancy and I practiced trying to get and couldn't.

"May I please speak to Mark?" My own voice had suddenly become so hoarse I had to clear my throat and cough a couple of times.

"Just a minute," she said, and I hoped she was Joyce, not Allison.

Suddenly Mark said, "Hello," and I jumped.

"Hi," I said. "It's me—Charlie."

"Hi."

"Mark, was that Joyce?" I asked.

"No. That was Allison."

I gritted my teeth. "Did she tell you that Andy is giving a party next Saturday? And she and Joyce are going to be there?"

"No."

"Oh. Well, Andy invited me to come." I tried taking a couple of deep breaths to make it easier. "And he said I could ask you to come to the party with me."

"OK."

That took me by surprise. "Oh," I repeated, wishing I knew another, more exciting word. "Well then, I'll see you at rehearsal, I guess. When I find out what time the party is, I'll let you know."

"OK."

It dawned on me why he wasn't more talkative. "Are your sisters in the room with you?"

"You got it."

"Never mind, Mark," I told him. "Just remember that it's important that your sisters go to the party. I'll tell you why later. I think we'll solve the problem of your sisters and my brothers at the same time."

"Fine."

I hung up and stared at the phone. Why wasn't dating easy and fun? This was torture. Maybe it was fun for everyone else. Maybe the problem was me.

I called Nancy to tell her about the party and found that she wasn't too happy, either.

"Jed wants me to wear his football sweater," she said. "And I don't want either the sweater or Jed."

"I thought you liked Jed."

"He's sort of like strawberry yogurt. You can get awfully tired of strawberry yogurt in a hurry."

"Nancy, I called to invite you to Andy's party. You don't have to bring Jed with you. You can invite someone else." I told her all about the party and why Andy was giving it.

Nancy perked up immediately. "Great news! And I know who I'll ask—Larry Hathaway! He's on the basketball team. He reminds me of Dustin Hoffman with long legs."

After about an hour, Mom came in and signaled that I had to get off the phone. I felt one hundred percent better. Nancy said this party had to work. There was no way anything could go wrong. And I agreed with her. That is, I hoped awfully hard she was right.

Chapter Seventeen

I didn't see Mark much during rehearsals because he was always with the chorus, and we weren't working together yet, but I thought about him a lot. And that was the problem. I should have been thinking about Billy.

He was still the shining apple of Mr. Gallen's eye. I would have liked Billy better as a baked apple. He didn't want to hold my hand during the opening scene. When he had the scene with Brooke where he had to kiss her, he yelled that he'd never kiss a girl and made a lot of yucky noises when his mother told him he'd have to. Half the guys in the auditorium volunteered to stand in for Billy during that scene, but all Billy did was sulk.

On Friday Mr. Gallen told us we'd have a run-through in costume. We all crowded around the rack where the costumes were hanging. We'd been measured for them, but this was the first time we had actually seen them. All except one of mine looked like potato sacks, but that one made up for the others. It was a long, red, sequined gown for the scene in which Vera and Mame make Agnes over. I loved it.

Mrs. Jennings, the costumer, and her assistants, two juniors, were handing out our costumes to us. Each one had a slip of paper pinned to it stating in which act and scene it would be worn. I carried mine to the dressing room, grabbed the costume I was supposed to wear in the opening scene, and pulled it over my head. That's as far as it went. I couldn't pull it down. Mrs. Jennings and her assistants were so busy that I couldn't get any of them to help. I was fumbling around the neckline trying to figure out what was the matter when Rita rescued me.

"There's something wrong with the hook on this," she said. "I pried it apart, but you'd better use a safety pin for now."

It was awfully crowded in there with all the girls in the first act getting into their costumes. As soon as someone was ready, she left. I took longer than anyone. There was something wrong with the left sleeve of the dress, too. It had all these little straight pins in it because it hadn't been finished. After I got stuck a few times, Rita made me take the dress off, and she quickly sewed it up, then handed it to me.

Brooke, looking gorgeous, was the last to leave. I called, "Wait! Can you pin the neck of this for me?"

"I'll do it," Mrs. Jennings said. Brooke hurried away.

I looked at myself in the mirror. Ugh! For some reason the dress drooped way down in front and looked even worse than I thought it would.

There was a knock on the door, and Billy opened it and peeked in. "You look terrible."

"Thanks." I gave another pull to the skirt and started for the door.

"My uncle said you should stay in the dressing room until he calls you."

"Why?" That darned skirt wouldn't hang right. I tugged at it again.

"Because that's the way it will be opening night. He wants us to get used to it."

"OK." I was still worrying about why that skirt was so weird as I sat on one of the folding chairs and waited.

In a few minutes the door flew open, and Rita yelled, "Hurry up, Charlie! Mr. Gallen is getting mad because you're taking so long!"

"But he said—" I began, and then I realized how dumb I'd been to listen to Billy. I just ran after Rita to my place at stage right.

"She's here," someone called, and Mr. Gallen snapped, "Let's get started!"

Billy looked as innocent as Rick at his worst and took my hand without a word of complaint.

"Pretty funny," I said. "Don't try anything else like that because from now on I'll be prepared for you."

Mrs. Yolinski attacked the piano keys, and Billy and I walked on stage.

I was in the middle of my opening speech when Mr. Gallen slapped the piano into silence and said, "What are you doing in that costume, Charlene?"

"It had 'Act One, Scene One' pinned on it, so I put it on," I said.

"No, it didn't," he answered. "You weren't paying attention. After Mrs. Jennings pinned those notes to the costumes, I personally double-checked them. You're wearing the maternity dress that Gooch wears in the last act."

"So that's why the skirt sags in front," I said, as everyone laughed. I felt my face growing warm enough to toast marshmallows.

"We don't have time for you to change," he said. "Just don't make that mistake in the future. Now, let's take it from the beginning."

Billy grinned at me. "Pretty good, huh?" he whispered.

I just shrugged. I was so angry I was working on keeping my temper. Billy looked puzzled. "Aren't you going to threaten me?"

"Why should I?"

"Because I got you in trouble."

I took a good, long look at Billy, and a lot of my anger went away. He was just a little kid. A mean little kid, but if I couldn't handle him, all my years of having brothers would have been wasted.

The piano came back to life, and I said, "Billy, let's do a really good job with this scene, and afterward we'll talk."

"About what?" He looked suspicious.

"About football," I said, then stepped on stage, pulling a very confused Billy along with me.

The scene went OK. "Get a little more into the Gooch character," Mr. Gallen told me. "Try for that wistful quality in your voice."

It wasn't until after the party scene that Mr. Gallen said we could break for a few minutes. I took a firm grip on Billy's shoulder and walked him away from the group to a couple of aisle seats in the shadowy back of the auditorium.

"You're going to yell at me," Billy said.

"No, I'm not," I said. "I'm going to ask you if you like football."

"Why?" His eyes were little slits as he stared at me.

"Because you might like to go to one of the high-school football games with me when this play is over. My brothers Rick and Adam are on the team. They're usually in the starting lineup."

"Uh—sure," Billy said. "Why do you want to take me?"

"Why not?" I said.

"You're not mad at me?"

"My brothers have played all sorts of tricks on me, and I guess I'm used to it," I said.

"Don't you get mad at your brothers?"

"Sure, but I love them all the same."

He squirmed in his seat. "You're not going to tell me you love me, too, are you? Because if you are, then don't. It would make me sick."

"I'm not going to."

"I don't understand you," Billy said.

"You don't have to. And I don't have to understand you. All we have to do is work well together and not play tricks on each other, since we want this play to be as good as we can make it."

"We do?"

"Sure we do."

"Now you're starting to sound like my uncle."

"That's because the musical means a lot to him. It's his job to see that it's successful."

"Would he get fired if it wasn't?"

"I don't think so, but he'd be unhappy."

"Now you sound like my mother."

"Billy," I said, "I've got enough problems without having to wonder what trick you'll think of next, and I'm trying to handle this in a grown-up, intelligent way."

Billy made a strangling sound. "You? Grown up and intelligent?"

"So, Billy," I continued, calmly refraining from throttling him, "I'm having this talk with you to explain the situation, to offer my friendship, and to try to get you to listen to reason. I don't want any more trouble during this play. OK?"

"Now you sound like my teacher," Billy said.

"You're right. I'm going to be myself. There is a spot in one of the scenes where it would be possible for Gooch to do something really terrible to Patrick right on stage in front of everybody."

"You wouldn't do that."

"Yes, I would." I turned and looked at him so intently that he leaned as far back in the seat as he could get. "Any questions?"

Billy nodded. "If I don't make any more trouble for you and you take me to a football game, can I sit on the bench with your brothers?"

"Of course not. But maybe, if I feel like it, I'll ask Rick and Adam to let you go into the locker room after the game. OK?"

"OK," he said, and he smiled at me. "I would have gotten tired of thinking up tricks pretty soon." He was off down the aisle before I could answer him.

Someone else slipped into the seat. Andy. "I heard part of that," he said. "Congratulations."

"Save the congratulations until we see if it works."

"I think it will. You laid it on the line for him. Maybe you could do the same thing with Rick and Adam."

"Do you think they'd take me seriously? Billy is smaller than I am, so I can make him listen."

Mr. Gallen was calling everyone onstage for the next scene. Andy got up, gave me a hand, and pulled me to my feet. "I hope you've got something more attractive than that dress to wear to my party tomorrow night," he said.

Tomorrow night!

I must have looked as scared as I felt because Andy said, "Relax. I've asked some of the kids in the play, so there'll be lots of people there you know. I can guarantee that you'll have a good time—at least until you and Mark leave the party."

For a moment I wished we'd never thought of that party idea.

"It's what you want, isn't it?" Andy asked, when I didn't say anything.

"Of course it is." I hoped I sounded as though I meant it.

Chapter Eighteen

Nancy phoned on Saturday to talk about Andy's party.

"Did you tell Mark your plan to sneak out of the party?"

"I sort of forgot."

"You haven't told him?"

"Nancy, when I phoned Mark to ask him to the party, his sisters were in the room, so he couldn't talk much, and afterward I guess I just forgot. I'd better tell him when he comes to pick me up. We can talk about it on the way to the party."

"You'd better talk fast," Nancy advised. "It's not that far from your house to Andy's."

From where I sat with the phone in my lap, I could see across the lawn to the side of Andy's house. There was a big maple tree between the

141

houses—the tree I used to climb to spy on the boys when they made a clubhouse on Andy's front porch. They would yell at me to get away because no girls were allowed.

My brothers were still pests, but Andy had certainly improved. I found myself smiling as I thought of him. Then I thought of Allison, and my smile disappeared. Well, what business was it of mine what Andy thought of Allison? I was interested in Mark. Right?

"It will work out," I told Nancy.

Later, when Rick and Adam weren't around, I told Mom.

There was a little wrinkle between her eyebrows, which meant she wasn't too sure she liked the idea. "Where do you and Mark plan to go?"

"I don't know. Maybe to a movie. Maybe to get something to eat."

"Wouldn't you have more fun at the party?"

I flopped on the sofa. "If we stay at the party, Adam and Rick won't leave us alone."

"I think you're exaggerating, Charlie. They're attempting to stand in for Dad. They're just going about it a little too seriously."

"But I'm not their responsibility, Mom!"

She thought a moment, then nodded. "All right. Maybe your plan will work out."

"It's OK with you if we leave the party?"

"Yes. However—"

She paused, and I said, "However what?"

"You might have such a good time at the party that you won't want to leave."

I didn't tell Mom that that thought had occurred to me. But when it had, I just closed my eyes and saw Mark and me, hand in hand, walking along the sand as the sun tinted the sky with streaks of red gold, and fingers of surf left trails of bubbles at our feet. Granted, where we live there isn't any beach or surf, and by the time we left the party the sun would be long gone from the sky; but I didn't know where to put us in my imagination, and the beach seemed as good a place as any. I looked up into Mark's eyes, but they were dark brown, and they were Andy's. And the face was Andy's, and the strong hand was Andy's.

"Wait a minute! Something's wrong," I whispered to myself, and squeezed my eyes so tightly shut that the picture vanished. When I looked again—very carefully—Mark was there, and Andy had gone. I decided to forget those mental images and just look forward to the party.

Rick couldn't believe that Andy had invited me. "He's lost his mind. Why would he invite a sophomore to his party?"

"He said he was asking a lot of the people working in the musical," Adam said. "Maybe he thought he'd hurt Charlie's feelings if he left her out."

Rick just shook his head. "Well, we can keep an eye on her tonight. She'll be right there under our noses."

"And you'll be under mine," I retorted.

Rick and Adam looked very uncomfortable as they stared at each other. I almost laughed. If they only knew what Andy and I had planned.

"Any other sophomores going to this party?" Rick asked me.

I shrugged. "Ask Andy."

"Maybe I won't go," Adam said. "It sounds like a dumb party."

Quickly I said, "Joyce and Allison Potter are going to be there."

Adam's eyes widened just a fraction. "On the other hand," he said, "I wouldn't want to hurt Andy's feelings."

I was so relieved I let out a long sigh, then clapped my hand over my mouth. But they were already making plans for the party and didn't pay any attention to me.

Mark was about twenty minutes late. By the time he arrived, I had a headache. "I waited until my sisters left," he said. "I didn't tell them I was going to Andy's party."

"Maybe I should have stayed home because they're going to be there," he added, as he walked into the living room.

"But we have to go to Andy's party!" I shouted.

He gave me a puzzled look. "Why are you so excited about it?

So I told him the plan.

"Well," he said after he thought a moment,

144

"I guess I'd like to see you without thinking that one of your brothers was about to jump me. Where will we go?"

"To a movie?"

"I haven't got that much money with me."

"We could get something to eat."

"There's usually a lot of food at a party. We probably won't be hungry."

I was beginning to wish that Mark had a little more imagination. Great looks weren't everything. "We could go for a walk." It was the only thing I could think of.

"Maybe we should just stay at the party."

"Mark," I said, "we can go to the mall. There's always something going on there on Saturday night."

"OK."

Mom came in. "You must be Mark Potter," she said, holding out her hand.

She chatted with Mark for a few minutes. When it was time for us to leave, she suggested that I wear a warmer coat. I knew she was thinking about my plan to leave the party.

"Have a good time," she said.

Famous last words. That party was *not* a good time.

Rick had decided to bring his own date, a girl named Lisa, who never let him out of her sight. Adam was talking to Brooke, but they became part of a threesome when Adam's former girlfriend Brenda showed up. Brenda's date, Tom, became very interested in Nancy, who didn't mind, because Larry, the guy she came with, got the hiccups and couldn't get rid of them. More and more people came, and I never did find out who Joyce was with. I guess I kept watching Andy. He hardly ever stopped dancing with Allison.

Finally he went to the kitchen for something, and I followed him. "I thought Rick was supposed to be with Allison," I said.

Andy shrugged. "Rick brought his own date."

"But it's not working out right!" I said.

Andy turned to face me, trying to juggle a stack of ice cube trays. "Sure it is, Charlie."

"I mean—"

"I don't think you know what you mean. Rick and Adam are busy. If you and Mark go on your way, they won't even notice."

"You mean now?" I asked. I wondered why I felt so awful.

"Now." Andy dumped the ice cubes into a bowl and left the kitchen.

"This party isn't any fun," I mumbled to myself. "I should be glad to leave." I went to find Mark.

"We have to go now?" Mark said. "They haven't even brought out all the food yet."

"We can get something to eat at the mall," I said.

Tom and Nancy brushed past us, and Nancy whispered in my direction, "I love older men!"

I watched them join the slow dancers. Allison had an arm practically wrapped around Andy's neck. "Let's get out of here, Mark," I said, "right this minute!" I pulled him outside.

As we hurried down the walk he said, "What are you so grouchy about?"

"I'm not grouchy," I snapped.

"It wasn't a bad party. My sisters pretended they didn't know me, so I was having a good time."

We started walking in the direction of the mall. By the time we had gone about six blocks and were standing on the corner of one of the major cross streets. My headache was getting worse and worse. I knew something was very wrong. I stopped and looked at Mark. I thought about how much I had wanted to date him, and suddenly I didn't want to anymore. Something boring had happened to Mark. He wasn't even as handsome as I had thought. There were a lot of guys who were more exciting.

Like Andy, for instance.

"Let's go back to the party," I said.

"What about your plan?" he asked.

"Forget it. It's not important now. But before we go back, I just want to stop in this drugstore and get some aspirin. I've got a terrible headache and maybe the pharmacist will give me a drink of water so I can take some right away."

"Sure," said Mark. We walked into the store, which was brightly lit with fluorescent lights.

The pharmacist was at the counter in back. There was another customer standing near him. We walked up to the counter. My head was really pounding.

"I'd like some aspirin, please," I said. Then I heard Mark gasp. Suddenly I realized that the man standing next to the pharmacist was not a customer at all! He was holding a gun and was stuffing money from the open cash register into a paper bag. The pharmacist stood stiffly beside him, his hands in the air.

"Don't anybody move," the robber snarled.

"We just wanted some aspirin," stammered Mark. "We'll go somewhere else—"

"Shut up! You heard me. Now get down on the floor, all of you!"

I have never been so terrified. Mark and I threw ourselves down on the floor. So did the pharmacist. Mark's legs are real long, though, and he accidentally hit a vitamin floor display with his foot. About forty jars of vitamins came crashing down and rolled across the floor in all directions.

"Idiot!" yelled the burglar. He was backing away from the counter toward the door with the bag full of money. "Now stay put, and nobody'll get hurt."

Just then, he stepped on some of the vitamin jars, and for a moment it seemed like he was on roller skates. He glided a little way down the aisle and then his feet flew straight up over his head. He came crashing down a few feet from where Mark and I lay. The gun flew out of his hands in our direction, and I grabbed it.

"Don't move!" I shouted, pointing the gun at the burglar. I don't think he was going anywhere, though, because he had fallen pretty hard, and he was moaning something about his shoulder.

"I'll call the police," said the pharmacist, getting up and running to his telephone.

Mark sat up. "I can't believe it," he said. "Is this for real?"

Before I could answer, the pharmacist returned. "The police are on their way," he said. "They should be here in a few minutes." He took the gun from me but kept it pointed at the guy on the floor.

He kept saying over and over how glad he was we had saved his life until the police arrived and found there weren't any bullets in the gun. Then he just grumbled a lot about having to pick up the jars of vitamins.

One of the policemen said to us, "We'll take your statements, and you can go home, or wherever you want to go."

"To a party," Mark said.

"We'll give you a lift," the officer said.

The policemen dropped us off in front of Andy's house. Somebody saw us and told everyone, and they all came out to see us climbing out of a police car. I realized we should have refused the ride and walked back.

It was too late. Adam and Rick got that "what-have-you-done" look, and I was afraid that nothing and no one—not Mom, not even Andy—could help me solve my brother problem now.

Chapter Nineteen

Adam stepped forward. He looked sort of like General Patton in that movie scene where he's in front of the flag addressing the troops.

"Whatever's happened, I can handle it," he said to the policeman who had gotten out of the car.

"There's nothing to handle."

"I mean whatever trouble my little sister has got into, I can—"

The policeman interrupted. "This is your little sister?"

"Yes," Adam said. I knew he was trying not to sound impatient. "I'd like to know what happened."

Allison came bouncing down the porch steps, Joyce right behind her. "What's happened, Mark?" she cried.

The policeman chuckled. "I'll leave you two to do the explaining," he said, then got back into the car. Before we could object, the car pulled away.

"Well, you see," I explained, "Mark and I went into this drugstore to get some aspirin for my headache." Just then, I realized my headache was gone. All of the excitement had made me forget about it.

"And the store was being robbed," Mark continued. "We sort of accidentally stopped the robbery."

"How could you accidentally stop a robbery?" Rick asked.

"Easy." I gave a long sigh. "Do we have to talk about it?"

"We want to know," demanded Rick.

"Well, just as the burglar was trying to get away with the money, I knocked over a floor display of vitamins," Mark said.

Allison's eyes grew wider and wider. "How did you manage that?"

Mark shrugged. "My foot kind of bumped it. Anyway, the robber tripped on the vitamins and fell down. Charlie grabbed his gun."

"You what?" Adam grabbed my shoulder, but I pushed his hand away.

"It was nothing," I said.

"You took on a robber with a gun, and you didn't even have a weapon?" Adam asked.

"I didn't actually take him on," I tried to explain.

"This is insane!" Allison said.

"No, this is Charlie," Rick said.

Andy laughed.

"We obviously can't let you out of our sight." Adam was stern.

I sighed. This was it, I thought. The complete end of my social life. From now on, my brothers would never leave me alone. No one would ever ask me out again.

Andy said, "Come back inside, everybody."

Mark went inside, but the last thing I wanted to do was go back to the party. My headache was starting to come back.

"No, thank you," I said, as formally as I could manage. I turned regally, stumbled over a bump in the walkway, and marched home.

Mom was writing a letter to Dad when I came in. "I'm going to do some homework," I told her.

She looked surprised. "What happened to the party?" She thought a moment. "I guess I should ask, what happened to Mark?" She put down her pen. "Judging from the unhappy look on your face I should begin by asking what happened to you, Charlie?"

After I told her, she put her arms around me and said, "Oh, honey, you might have been hurt!"

"I didn't do it on purpose, Mom. It just happened."

"Never mind. Tell me why you didn't want to go back to the party."

"Well, for one thing, I have a headache." I dropped to the floor and sat cross-legged. "Mom, it's really tragic. Now Adam and Rick will never let me out of their sight."

"You handled a robber without any trouble, it seems. Is it that much harder handling your brothers?"

That made me think of Mr. Hartman, so I told Mom about the journals he told everyone to keep.

"It sounds like a good approach," she said. "Mr. Hartman is right. It's up to you, Charlie, to work out this problem with Rick and Adam."

I had to smile. "You mean I can't always call for Mama."

"Do you want to?"

"No," I said.

She reached down and took my hand and gave it a little squeeze. "I think you can work it out so that your next date with Mark will be more successful."

"Mom, I don't care if I ever go out with Mark again. In fact, I won't." I got to my feet. "But I did find out something—that if I really like a guy, I can think of lots to talk about."

"I thought you said you *didn't* like Mark that much."

"I'll tell you more later." I had to get that notebook and write everything out. I had the feeling it would help me decide what to do.

Chapter Twenty

Nancy came over the next afternoon. "I really like him," she said, throwing herself across my bed and smiling at the ceiling.

"Tom does seem to be nice," I said.

Nancy sat up. "Tom who? Oh, I don't mean Tom. Brenda and Adam got very cold to each other, and Brenda went back to Tom. Tom forgot my name inside of half a second. So I helped Larry put a paper bag over his head, and his hiccups finally went away."

"I thought Larry was nice," I said.

"What are you going to do about Mark?" Nancy asked.

"Forget him. I got awfully tired of him in a hurry."

"We'll find you someone else," Nancy said.

"That's OK." I sat down next to Nancy. "Tell me more about who did what at the party."

"Well, Brooke told me she invited Adam to the cast party, and he said he'd go with her. And Rick and Allison danced a lot together, and he seemed to like her, and—"

"Wait a minute!" I interrupted Nancy. "I thought Andy and Allison were together."

"Oh, they were at first, but then Lisa got interested in Andy. You know something, Charlie? Andy is really very nice."

"I know," I said, wishing I could keep from sounding so gloomy.

Nancy gave me a quick look. "Let's not talk anymore about the party," she said. "Let's talk about—well—I know! Let's do our history homework." Which shows what sacrifices a really good friend makes for another.

Doing homework on Sunday afternoon is almost a shock to the system, so I was relieved when we finished and Nancy went home. I walked out on the porch with her, watching her leave. Then I glanced over at Andy's house. Sitting out on the porch in the cold were Adam, Rick, and Andy.

An awful lot of thoughts went through my head: Andy telling me I should talk to Adam and Rick, and Mom telling me I could take care of things myself, and Mr. Hartman telling the class we had to work out our own solutions.

"OK," I said under my breath, "now's the time."

I got my jacket. Then I walked across the lawn, right up to Andy's porch, and sat down with them.

"Is it time for dinner?" Rick asked.

"Mom didn't send me to get you."

"What's up?" asked Adam.

"I want to talk to you."

"Can it wait until later?" he asked. "We're discussing something important right now."

"This is important."

"Well, then shoot," said Rick.

Everyone was quiet. Andy was leaning back against the porch railing. He was watching me closely. I took a deep breath.

"It has to do with my social life."

"What's wrong with your social life?" asked Adam.

"You're what's wrong with it," I said. "You and Rick are driving me crazy! I know you care about me, and I know you feel that with Dad away, I need some kind of protection. And I understand. I really do. But I'm fifteen years old! I'm not a little girl anymore. I can handle any problems that come up on my own. I don't need you to follow me around when I go out, just to make sure that I'm OK."

Adam put his hand on my shoulder. "Look, sis," he said solemnly, "we really do care about you. That's why we look after you the way we do. We realize you're fifteen now, but that's still pretty young. If Dad were home, he'd—"

"But that's my whole point, Adam! I don't

even need Dad to look after me anymore. I'm quite capable of looking after myself!"

Rick and Adam glanced at each other. "I guess we have been pretty rough on you," Adam admitted. "But it's been for your own good."

"I could go out with someone you'd approve of," I told them, "but that's beside the point. What's important is that *I* decide for myself who I'm going out with. I'm serious, guys. Do you hear what I'm saying?"

Rick grinned. "Yeah. I didn't like the way having to baby-sit you cut into my dating time, anyway."

"So does that mean I can go out now without the two of you breathing down my neck and intimidating all my dates?"

There was a long silence. I was relieved to see that they were taking me seriously.

"Well," Adam finally said, "I can't guarantee that we won't slip up once in awhile and start worrying about you again, but if you really want us to, we can try to remember that you are growing up and that, most of the time, you can take care of yourself. I guess Dad will have to realize that, too, when he gets home."

"Want to be friends, Charlie?" Rick asked. I had to smile back.

Just then Mom appeared on the front porch. "There you are," she called. "Dinner's ready."

"Let's go," Adam said. "I'm starved."

Rick was the first one off the porch. Adam

followed. Andy got to his feet and held down a hand to me, pulling me up.

"It looks as though you'll have your chance with Mark now," Andy said.

"I don't want Mark." I told Andy as I looked into his eyes. They were beautiful eyes, and they were looking into mine. Just a trace of a smile flickered on his lips. I lifted my chin. We were standing so close together that if I leaned forward just a little, just a very little. . . .

"Charlie!" Rick yelled. "Hurry up! You know Mom won't let us eat until you get here!"

"There's one more thing I can do," I told Andy. "Not because I have to but because I want to. I can date someone Rick and Adam would approve of because he's their friend."

I waited, but Andy didn't say a word. He just kept looking at me with that funny little smile that made me wish I hadn't opened my mouth.

"Charlie! I'm hungry! Run!" Rick shouted.

I did.

Chapter Twenty-One

All during dinner Adam kept studying me as though he were seeing me for the first time. Rick looked at me kind of funny, too. He even told me my hair was looking better than it usually did. But I kept thinking about how I had practically thrown myself at Andy, and I wondered how I'd face him the next day at rehearsal.

I couldn't even tell Nancy what I'd done, but I could put it in my journal. I took one page to write about how I had talked to Adam and Rick and how that part of my problem seemed to be solved. I wouldn't really know until I went out with someone again. And I wrote that there was only one person I really wanted to date, but that I might have ruined any chance of that.

* * *

I didn't know what would happen next. I kept my mind on what was going on in class and thought about the work we'd be doing in rehearsal.

The rehearsal that evening was like any other. Everyone made a few mistakes, but we were getting better. I thought about poor, dateless Agnes Gooch. We had a lot in common. I really began to relate to her. Afterward Mr. Gallen told me I was doing a fine job.

"Will your family be here on opening night?" he asked.

"My mom and my brothers will," I said.

"They'll be proud of you, Charlene," he said. "Who knows? Someday you may sing professionally."

"That's one of my goals."

"You've been very good with Billy, too," he told me, dropping his voice and looking around carefully to make sure he wasn't overheard. "I know he can be difficult at times, even if he is my nephew, but you've brought out the best in him. Probably by offering him your friendship."

More likely by bribery and threats, I thought, but I just smiled and didn't say anything.

After rehearsal, I wished for the first time that my brothers were coming to get me. I walked with Andy to his car, talking about the play and the costumes—anything to cover up the way I felt.

Andy drove out of the school parking lot and said, "I didn't come over last night because

I wanted to talk to you when Rick and Adam weren't around."

"It's OK. You don't have to talk to me."

"It's going to be very hard to ask you for a date if I don't talk."

I squeezed my fingers together in my lap and stared down at them. My face was burning. "Andy, you've been very nice to me, and I appreciate it, and I think we should just forget what I said to you yesterday."

"I wasn't just being nice to you. I had an ulterior motive."

For the first time I looked at him. Passing lights flickered over his face, and I thought again how handsome he was.

"What ulterior motive?"

"It's this way. You thought of me as just another big brother, and you had your mind set on going out with Mark Potter, so I knew you wouldn't go out with me if I asked."

"But—"

"Just listen," Andy said. "I helped along the Mark Potter thing. I knew you wouldn't stay interested in anyone that dull. And Mr. Hartman helped me with the big brother thing."

"You mean Mr. Hartman knew you wanted to ask me out?"

"Nope. But he taught us those mental exercises, and that's what I did. I put us together in my mind, and it worked. I was just waiting until you let me know you were ready."

Once I would have given Andy a big sisterly

hug, but suddenly I was so shy I couldn't even look at him.

For the first time I noticed that Andy had parked the car in his driveway. "Come on," he said. "I'll walk you to your door."

He took my hand as we crossed the lawn and went up the porch steps. Then he stopped in front of the closed door, turned, and put both hands on my shoulders. "Charlie," he said, "there's a new movie opening in town on Saturday night. Would you like to see it with me?"

"I'd love to, Andy."

Just then the porch light zapped on, and I blinked in all that brightness. Rick opened the door and stepped outside. "Oh, it's you," he said. "I thought I heard someone out here."

"Go back in," Andy told him. "And turn out that dumb light."

Rick looked surprised. "Don't tell me you're going to give Charlie another singing lesson."

"Go on, Rick," I said. "It's really none of your business, but Andy and I are making plans for Saturday night."

Rick looked surprised.

Andy turned and glared at him.

"OK, old buddy," Rick said. "I guess you know what you're doing." As he stepped inside, he poked his head out. "Remember all the crazy things that happen on Charlie's dates."

"This time will be different," Andy said.

The moment Rick and his thousand-watt porch light disappeared Andy said, "Don't pay attention to Rick. Saturday is going to be a very special day."

"And nothing crazy is going to happen," I promised.

Fortunately, I was right. Nothing crazy happened on Saturday night. Andy and I had what was probably the world's most ordinary date. The car didn't break down, the police weren't involved, no robberies occurred, and my brothers were delightfully absent throughout the entire evening. We went to a movie, and afterward to get some ice cream. I even got home on time. It was wonderful!

What was especially nice about the evening, though, was that I had absolutely no trouble talking to Andy. I didn't need to memorize lists of conversational topics or quiz him about his car or family. It just happened. From the moment he picked me up until the moment he kissed me good night on my front porch, we talked and talked. Although Andy and I have lived next door to each other most of our lives, there was a lot I didn't know about him.

We've seen a lot of each other over the last few months. I can't believe it's already spring! We worked together on the school musical, of course, and we also did some cross-country skiing, which was fun. But most of the time we spent just hanging out together, doing our homework or watching TV.

I guess Mom was right. To enjoy going out

with someone, all I had to do was just relax and be myself. But for that to happen, it took a special guy. Someone warm and relaxed, who wouldn't expect me to be clever or charming all the time. Someone who would like me just the way I am.

That is Andy. And he was right there, all the time.

You'll fall in love with all the Sweet Dream romances. Reading these stories, you'll be reminded of yourself or of someone you know. There's Jennie, the *California Girl*, who becomes an outsider when her family moves to Texas. And Cindy, the *Little Sister*, who's afraid that Christine, the oldest in the family, will steal her new boyfriend. Don't miss any of the Sweet Dreams romances.

☐ 14019	**P.S. I LOVE YOU** Barbara P. Conklin	$1.95
☐ 20325	**THE POPULARITY PLAN** Rosemary Vernon	$1.75
☐ 20327	**LAURIE'S SONG** Debra Brand	$1.75
☐ 14020	**PRINCESS AMY** Melinda Pollowitz	$1.95
☐ 20326	**LITTLE SISTER** Yvonne Green	$1.75
☐ 20324	**CALIFORNIA GIRL** Janet Quin-Harkin	$1.75
☐ 14022	**GREEN EYES** Suzanne Rand	$1.95
☐ 14021	**THE THOROUGHBRED** Joanna Campbell	$1.95
☐ 22991	**COVER GIRL** Yvonne Green	$1.95
☐ 22992	**LOVE MATCH** Janet Quin-Harkin	$1.95
☐ 20787	**THE PROBLEM WITH LOVE** Susan Mendonca	$1.75
☐ 20788	**NIGHT OF THE PROM** Debra Spector	$1.75
☐ 22607	**ALL'S FAIR IN LOVE** Jeanne Andrews	$1.95
☐ 22683	**SECRET IDENTITY** Joanna Campbell	$1.95

Buy them at your local bookstore or use this handy coupon for ordering:

Bantam Books, Inc., Dept. SD, 414 East Golf Road, Des Plaines, Ill. 60016

Please send me the books I have checked above. I am enclosing $_____ (please add $1.25 to cover postage and handling). Send check or money order—no cash or C.O.D.'s please.

Mr Mrs Miss _____

Address _____

City _____ State Zip _____

SD-10/82

Please allow four to six weeks for delivery. This offer expires 4/83

Sweet Dreams Diary™

(01456-0) 5¼″ × 7⅝″ $5.95

Now you can have a place to record all your dreams, secret desires and special feelings. The SWEET DREAMS DIARY gives you the perfect opportunity to jot it all down. Plus, it's filled with sayings about love and friendship, poems, and astrological information. The diary is spiral-bound, which makes it easy to write in, no matter where you are.

So order your copy of the SWEET DREAMS DIARY today—and let your friends know about it. In the years to come, you'll be able to look back in your diary and see which of your dreams have come true!

— — — — — — — — — — — — — — — —

Read these great new *Sweet Dreams* romances on sale soon:

( ) **#25 HER SECRET SELF by Rhondi Villot** (On sale October 15 * #22543-X * $1.95)
Joanne enjoys doing impressions of famous people, but her impersonations are making her miserable. Even her boyfriend has gotten tired of her role-playing and has started dating gorgeous Christiana. Then Joanne meets Cliff, the class president, and he seems really interested in her—until he is stung by one of her imitations. Will Joanne's illusions keep her from ever finding real-life happiness?

( ) **#26 THIS MUST BE MAGIC by Marian Woodruff** (On sale October 15 * #22692-4 * $1.95)
It's the junior class genie week and Kerrie's friends have gotten together to buy her dreamy Mike in the genie auction. Working together with Mike in hopes of winning awards for best couple, best stunts and best costume at the school parade at the end of the week, Kerrie realizes just how much she has been missing paying so much attention to school work and not enough to boys. But can she ever possibly hope to lure Mike away from his beautiful girlfriend Marcy?

( ) #27 TOO YOUNG FOR LOVE by Gailanne Maravel
(On sale November 15 * #22681-9 * $1.95)
It looks like Tom and Killy's friendship is turning into
romance . . . but then Tom finds out Killy's two years
younger than the other kids in school. Killy is miserable,
until she leaves the whole mess behind for a glamorous
vacation in Italy. When she gets back, she feels sophisticated
and grown up. But will Tom think so, too?

( ) #28 TRUSTING HEARTS by Jocelyn Saal (On sale
December 15 * 23058-0 * $1.95)
Kathy's overjoyed with her new romance, until her boyfriend
Dean starts resenting the long hours she puts in at her job
at the animal hospital. Suddenly, their love seems about
to fall apart. Kathy would be lost without Dean, but she
loves her new job just as much. Will she have to make a
choice between them?

Buy these books at your local bookstore or use this handy
coupon for ordering: